BEHIND GLASS

ELLE SCOTT

BOOKS BY ELLE SCOTT

THE INCANDESCENT SERIES
Ray of Light
Harbour of Light
Symphony of Light

SHADOW GUARDIANS
Ever Marked
… plus more to come

BE A PART OF THE TEAM
www.facebook.com/groups/ellescottstreetteam

Dedicated to all those friends who I rarely see,
but when we get around to that long awaited catch up,
it's like we've never been apart.

Eden

"Sometimes, what feels like the beginning, is actually the end."

She didn't know his name. But she knew his face... she knew his eyes. Blue. Unwavering. Bloodshot.

Whenever Eden drifted to sleep, his gem-like irises were the first thing she'd see. It was a cloudy vision from a broken and old memory. Something that felt close enough to touch, but always just out of reach.

He was gone because of her, or so she believed. She felt it in her bones. Eden knew she'd made a mistake, somehow, somewhere in a time she couldn't remember.

And, right before she found out the truth, she made another one. Monumental.

From the outside, the exact moment of her second mistake was easy to pinpoint. It started when she used the powers she didn't know she had. But looking a little deeper, it began with a memory. Small yet significant. Like a tiny spark caught a breath of air and rolled into a light so fierce it could blind even the sun.

That night was seared into her mind; one she would never forget.

The evening started the way it had for the last six years; with Eden's parents asking her the same set of questions. Her answers were always the same... every night until then.

She sat in her favorite armchair. It was black for the most part, except for the seat which was re-covered with tartan flannel. Eden had chosen it two years ago because it reminded her of herself—worn at the edges and patched together.

"What's your name?" Eden's dad, Alistair Howard, sat forward in his brown leather chair opposite her. The tip of his pen pressed down on his pad of paper. Ready. He was handsome, rugged yet poised. But, at thirty-four, he was too young to be Eden's biological father.

Eden inhaled long and slow, then replied, "Eden Howard."

"When's your birthday?" Alistair asked, already writing.

"In a few days. October fifth."

In the corner of the room, underneath the dull light of a lamp, Eden's mom, Lacey, sat in her own chair. It was mustard-yellow with faded mahogany legs and a long provincial back. She was pretending to read Hemingway, or Orwell, or King. But Eden knew she was listening just as intently as Alistair, if not more.

"What do you remember before your twelfth birthday?" asked Alistair.

Ah, the big one. The main one. The pièce de résistance.

"Nothing," Eden replied, flatly.

Alistair glanced up, glaring over the rims of his

black-framed glasses. She knew exactly what his stare meant. *Don't play games, Eden, tell the truth.*

Eden sighed. She'd gotten sick of the monotonous interrogation years ago. It made her feel like she was going a little crazy. Eden wanted to move on from the lack of memory and live her life like she was a normal seventeen-year-old. But, at the same time every day, her own desire to remember propelled her into the living room every evening to watch her dad write down her repetitive answers.

He was right to glower though, if Eden said she remembered nothing prior to her twelfth birthday, that would be a lie. There *was* something. Like always, she remembered—*him* and those eyes.

Her lips lifted into a half-smile, half-grimace. "Okay, fine. I remember standing behind a glass wall and seeing someone."

"Mm-hmm," Alistair mumbled, scribbling onto his paper. "What does he look like?"

The follow-up questions were just as tedious as the lead-up. Eden slouched into her chair and pinched a strand of hair. Studying the fibers, she twisted the hair around her fingers. "He's the same height as me... has dark hair like me too."

"Anything else noticeable about his hair?" Alistair asked the question casually, but hearing the words made Eden wince. He was preempting her answers. He'd heard it all a thousand times before too. He knew her words before she said them.

Eden opened her fingers and watched her hair untwist itself. Out of the corner of her eye, the white tendril bounced against her cheek. "He had the same silver streak through his hair. Like mine, but denser. It ran over his ear all the way to the nape of his neck."

She swept her palm over the side of her head, wondering what he would look like now, six years later. Her thoughts immediately fell into the darkest places of her mind. *He's probably dead.*

The vision of his face haunted her. She didn't just recite it every night for her parents, it followed her everywhere; in her dreams, when she woke, when she ate caramel. It was the one and only thing she could remember before her twelfth birthday and, ever since the memory had surfaced, she could hardly think of much else.

But her parents didn't know the full memory, they didn't know the other details. No, there were some things she hadn't told them... The blood that pooled across the mystery boy's shoulder. The desperation in his eyes. The way he screamed her name. And they would never know how her chest tightened like a boxer's fist at the thought of him.

"What else?" Alistair prompted, snapping Eden from her trance.

Lacey nonchalantly reached for her tea, still staring intently at the unturned pages of her book. As she slid her fingers along the mug, she dared a brief glance Eden's way. When she noticed her daughter watching, Lacey quickly averted her gaze and sipped her tea.

Eden finally answered her dad, "The color of his skin was a little lighter than caramel."

Her eyes wandered to the shadows between the dull light of the lamps in the room. The room was cozy any other time of day. During the question time though, Eden always felt claustrophobic. Eden swallowed hard and fell forward, her elbows finding her knees.

"Come on, Eden," Lacey finally spoke. "You can do better than that. Do we have to ask you every single little detailed question? Can't you just say what you know?"

Alistair fidgeted in his seat, gesturing with his pen. "Lacey, please. Give her time. The best parts come when she isn't rushed." His eyes turned to her once more, his voice becoming extra soft. "Go on, Eden. Tell us what you remember."

Eden knew they wanted more. But remembering *him* felt like torture. Could they not tell? Or did they just not care? Both questions hurt to even consider.

She lifted herself and folded her feet underneath her backside to sit on her ankles. Faking a smile, she asked, "What's for dessert?"

Lacey rolled her eyes.

"When we've finished, you can go to the corner store and get whatever you want. Just humor us, for a few more minutes." Alistair's voice had this deep vibrato to it, like an electric cello. It was warm and commanding at the same time.

Eden closed her eyes, daring herself to look at the boy's face once more. When she opened them again, she finally said, "His chin. It sticks out like it's too big for his face."

She smiled then as a knowing sensation filled her. It was a joke, she thought, between her and the boy. Which meant they were close. They cared about each other. She didn't say that out loud though. Not to her parents, not to anyone. She wanted to keep it private, like the way she felt when she saw the mystery boy's distress behind the glass wall that separated them. It was something between them, and them only.

"What color are his eyes?" Alistair asked next.

That answer was easy. Eden smiled wider. "Blue. Aqua, to be exact. Like Lake Louise in summer."

Lacey hastily placed her mug on the coffee table, its contents splashing from the movement. Alistair swung around to meet her astonished gaze. Eden blinked. She'd seen that look from them before.

Snapping her book shut, Lacey's stare swiveled to her daughter. "Honey, when have you seen Lake Louise?"

"We went there a few years ago... for a holiday." Eden frowned as they gawked at her with their lowered brows and widened eyes. "We kayaked... I ran my fingertips over the water."

Lacey gasped then. A glistening tear slipped from her eye and rolled down her cheek. "Oh my God!"

"Eden?" Alistair was calmer. He licked his lips as he readjusted his glasses. "We've never been to Lake Louise."

"Yes, we have..." Eden paused.

"When?" Breathless, Lacey's whole body shook with the small word.

Eden's heart quickened, breath suddenly rushing in and out of her lungs. Her eyes began searching the room for answers, as if she might actually find them outside of her mind. And somehow, in that moment, something changed. Like a dusty light bulb switching on, a spark lit inside her.

A new memory emerged. Something more than a missing boy. Deep down, she knew the moment had changed her life.

Eden inhaled as unexpected tears tumbled down her cheeks. She looked between her parents and, with a voice that sounded different from her own, she answered, "When I was eleven. I went to Lake Louise when I was *eleven*!"

Eden

Eden's second mistake was clear before the night was over.

"That deserves an éclair, right?" Eden hurled herself out of her chair before her dad had finished writing the new information. Her feet bounced off the floorboards as she slid through the living room archway.

"Eden?" Alistair dropped his notepad and pen, scrambling to follow her. "Rules!"

Her hand paused at the front door before wrapping her fingers around the knob. She sighed. "I know the rules."

"Well then?"

Eden looked over her shoulder to see Alistair grab her black beanie from the coat rack. He flung it in her direction. Catching it, Eden frowned. "I can be inconspicuous without covering myself up."

"The streak in your hair is different, it draws attention," Lacey said, joining her husband's side.

"Just wear it."

"And this." Alistair held up his finger, then spun on his heels and sprinted to the study door.

The study was a room like any other, except for the fact Eden was rarely allowed in it. Alistair was protective about his room, almost obsessively so. Eden wondered, at times, if there was something he was hiding in there.

Alistair pressed his thumb against the small scanning pad above it. He slipped inside and shut the door behind him.

Eden kneaded her fingertips along the beanie's edge and eyed Lacey, who gave a forced smile and shrugged. She threw her thumb at the study door. "Him and his gadgets."

It was her attempt at bringing light to the situation. Eden knew that Lacey loved her, but every now and then her warmth was decidedly less than Alistair's. In those moments, the fact that they weren't her real parents became painfully obvious.

Alistair opened the door with a small enough gap to fit through. Eden darted her eyes, but he was too quick—always too quick—for her to catch a glimpse of anything interesting. He walked toward her with purpose and latched a watch around her wrist. "Patrol begins as soon as the sun sets, don't be caught out there."

Patrol. Those nasty little drones that scanned the streets, beaming their lights on anyone who dared linger when night fell. The curfew was for the safety of all humanity, or so they were told. Eden could never quite understand why night was more dangerous than daytime.

"Have I ever?" Eden replied, turning back to the door.

"Take Zahra with you," Lacey added urgently.

Eden grabbed the handle and looked over her shoulder. "Do I ever go anywhere without her?"

As Eden swung the door open, Alistair rushed forward. "Restate the rules please, so we know you understand."

She frowned in frustration. But then, she softened. They weren't her biological parents but their loving concern was just as authentic—and annoying—as the real thing. It wasn't as though she was trying to be rebellious or even yearning for some independence. It was a dangerous world; she knew that. But sometimes, just sometimes, Eden wished they could trust her to do the right thing. She *always* did the right thing. She *always* followed those damn rules.

"Rule one: be inconspicuous."

Alistair wagged a finger at the beanie in her grasp. He pried it from her reluctant hands and placed it onto her head. Eden glanced at Lacey as Alistair carefully tucked her streak out of sight. Lacey shrugged, some warmth lighting her eyes.

"Rule two?" he asked, stepping back.

"Always take a friend outside." Eden lifted her hands to the sides of the beanie and looked between her adoptive parents. "And rule three is to come home if a memory surfaces."

Lacey moved closer to Eden and placed a hand on her shoulder. With steel eyes, she said, "That's the most important one."

"You guys worry too much," Eden said, shrugging herself free. Her parents' over-protectiveness almost made her forget about the new memory she'd just acquired. Almost. She stepped back through the doorway into the seventh-floor hallway and gave a cheesy grin. "I'll be back with treats."

Alistair's unamused gaze bored into her, and just before she closed the door, he warned, "Don't do anything to draw attention to yourself!"

Eden adjusted her beanie as she rode the elevator down from level seven to level three. Smiling to herself, she closed her eyes and let the new memory replay. A kayak bobbed silently on the lake as she dipped her fingertips into the icy water. A sense of excitement bubbled within, a knowing feeling that something important had just happened... that she'd just done something significant.

The memory was from a time where people could walk the streets at any moment of day, whether the sky was occupied by sun or moon. It was a time before the curfew, before the strict laws, before fear had spread through every person and every home. Eden didn't know how she knew it, but she knew. The knowledge sat deep in her bones.

It was a belief that demons had caused the panic. According to most people, they roamed the pavement at night, hunting anyone who dared to walk in the darkness. Eden wasn't like most people though, and there was always this nagging feeling that demons were just a myth—an elaborate lie to control the masses and keep them placated and compliant. She would often find herself standing at the edge of the kitchen fire escape, looking up into the smog-filled night sky, watching the drones scan the streets for signs of life as an overwhelming urge to dance in the moonlight tickled her heels. But still, the rumors of glowing eyes and strange abilities were enough to keep her obedient.

The elevator doors opened. The thought of telling Zahra about her new memory made Eden's heart flip. She stuffed her hands in her pockets and stepped into the corridor. Swallowing, she forced the excitement down. Zahra had this strange knack for sensing Eden's emotions, she didn't need to give it all away.

Beside the silver letters, *3A*, Eden rapped her knuckles. As she waited, she dug her fingertips around the space between her shoulder blade and spine. Her back always ached when she remembered things. It would be weird if it wasn't so normal.

The first time, it was foggy glass and a blurry vision of *his* shape behind it. The next time, it was *his* face and the exquisitely painful feeling that came with it. Then, a new memory of a boat and a lake. But a different feeling. Joy.

The smallest of smiles lifted the edges of Eden's mouth. A flurry of footsteps echoed behind the door she stood in front of. Before she had the chance to check her emotions, it swung open and Zahra burst through. A girl with long bleached curls against brown skin stood in the doorway. Zahra wore ripped jeans and her high-tops were laced with rainbow threads. A black choker hugged her neck. Her amber eyes gave Eden the once-over, and after noticing Eden's smile, she gave one of her own.

Zahra came into Eden's life almost immediately as soon as Alistair and Lacey brought Eden home when she was twelve. Kid Jane Doe from the hospital. Eden couldn't even remember her own name and there Zahra was, introducing herself. They did everything together: sneaking to the conservatory on the roof after dark, people watching from the front steps of the building during the day, and running to the corner bakery for dessert in that small space in between.

"I knew it was you!" Zahra beamed, throwing her arms wide.

Eden froze under the warm embrace. At once, all too aware of her over-sized hoodie, bland jean shorts, and white tennis shoes. Next to Zahra's talent for style, Eden felt a little subpar. Sucking it up, she returned her friend's hug with a chuckle. "Well, duh. I'm here all the time."

Inside the apartment, Zahra's twin brother leaned over the sofa, arching his back to see her through the doorway. His amber eyes twinkled at the sight of Eden. "Hey, E*eee*ds."

Kobe was very good-looking. He had a buzz cut

and a strong jawline. His skin was slightly darker than Zahra's, which made his eyes stand out like gems.

"Hey, Kobe." Still under Zahra's hold, Eden lifted her hand to give a lazy wave.

Kobe raised his hand in the same manner, unconsciously copying Eden's movements. She smiled. Zahra often called him "Mimic," because of his copycat habit.

Finally releasing Eden, Zahra shuffled back with a long sigh, leaving Eden standing in the corridor feeling slightly cold from the sudden disappearance of body warmth.

"Are you gonna invite the girl in?" Kobe lifted an eyebrow in amusement, and the crescent scar that cut through it became more pronounced. She'd asked him once how he got it, but Kobe dodged the question by playfully asking her why she'd only ever eat caramel-tasting sweets.

As she studied his dancing scar, the spot underneath Eden's left shoulder blade twinged. She winced and pressed her fingertips into the ache. "I'm on a food hunt, actually. Wanna come?"

Kobe glanced at Zahra, touching his own back. He climbed over the sofa like a monkey. "Do you have a sore back? Did you get a new memory, Eeds?"

Zahra spun to face her brother, her long tight curls gaining air as she moved. "Kobe!" she scolded, before turning back to Eden with an apologetic smile. "I didn't tell him what you said about your backaches, I swear."

"It's okay." Eden waved her arm in a semicircle toward the elevator. "You coming? Curfew won't wait."

Nodding profusely, Zahra stepped into the hall, practically slamming the door on her brother. As they hurried for the elevator, she said, "I'm really sorry, Eden. He's nosy sometimes. I promise I only slightly mentioned the thing about your sore back and memories."

Eden shrugged as they entered the elevator and rolled her shoulders extra hard. "You're twins, I expect you to tell him things. It's really okay."

"Are you going to tell me what you've remembered?" Zahra said, eyeing Eden's movements.

Eden gave her a sly side-smile. "It's a big one... I think."

Zahra grinned and clapped her hands with glee. "Well, don't leave me hanging, girl, tell me everything."

"Okay, okay. I'm on a boat..." Eden closed her eyes and let her mind wander. It was different telling Zahra things compared to the nightly questioning. There was no pressure, just friendship. "No, it's not a boat, it's a kayak I think. I'm at Lake Louise. The water is at its bluest, it's clear and calm."

Zahra's eyes rounded. "Lake Louise?"

She opened her eyes as the elevator doors revealed the foyer. "Yes," Eden replied.

The entrance of their apartment building had an old, charming feel. A bronze chandelier with five missing bulbs hung from the lofted ceiling while industrial-style lamps and mirrors lined an exposed red-bricked wall. When Zahra and Eden were younger they'd try to guess what the building had been before: an illegal dance club, an upscale vet, or a funky restaurant where they only served spaghetti and meatballs? Then, Kobe discovered that it had been a factory for producing feather pillows and the game died with the mystery.

As the girls walked toward the sliding glass doors, half of the building's occupants seemed to be making their way inside right at that moment. Remembering her parents' rule to stay inconspicuous, Eden subconsciously tugged her beanie down to her eyebrows. She weaved and dodged their neighbors.

In contrast, Zahra smiled warmly at those they passed, using first names with her almost pretentious greetings.

"So," Zahra huffed after pushing her way outside and onto the sidewalk. "Tell me more. Who were you with?"

Eden's smile faded; she hadn't gotten that far into the memory. As they walked side by side down the Brooklyn street, her hand instinctively reached for her hair. She twisted her silver streak around her fingers... thinking... straining.

A kayak. Lake Louise. What else?

The water had been cool as it lapped around her fingertips. Blue skies stretched above her, while around her walking tracks and trees reached for the sun. Behind her, there'd been... someone.

Eden opened her mouth to reply but shut it again immediately. She wanted to say a name; it was on the tip of her tongue.

"Never mind," Zahra said, seeing the struggle on Eden's face. She steered Eden into the bakery. "Don't push it."

Eden nodded, frustrated with herself. The instant she stepped into the bakery and the sweet smell of sugary things filled her senses, her excitement returned. She headed straight to the selection of éclairs in the Bain Marie.

"I've been to Lake Louise," Zahra stated, moving beside Eden. She bent down and rested her forehead against the glass, eyes hungry.

"When?" Eden asked, wondering if she should get the custard or the caramel. Who was she kidding, she'd get the caramel, like always.

Zahra straightened tall, her nose crinkling with thought. Her yellow irises flitted between Eden's. "About seven years ago."

Eden's heart flipped. "When you were eleven?"

Zahra chewed on the inside of her mouth, causing her bottom lip to disappear at its edge. "Yeah."

Frowning, Eden turned her attention back to the éclairs. "Have you told me about it before? Maybe it isn't my memory after all. Maybe I'm just remembering something you told me. Maybe I'm going crazy."

But the feeling she had with the vision, the coolness of the water, the excitement in her heart, that had to have been real. Right?

"No, Eden. It's your memory, too—" Zahra began.

The door chimed and Eden's heart pounded again. A sudden pang ran over her shoulders and she hunched over, trying to release the pain. It'd never been that bad before. Her insides swirled as adrenaline flooded her veins. Something wasn't right. It wasn't just the memory making her ache this time. The person who just entered the bakery, they weren't supposed to be there. Instinctively, she took a deep breath and arched her head to the door.

Standing in the doorway was a man, his wild eyes panning the store. Average height, late-twenties, oily hair that draped the sides of his face. He was otherwise ordinary if it weren't for the machete in his grip.

Spotting the bakery owner, he raised the weapon.

"Oy!" the man yelled.

The owner, startled by the intrusion, dropped a loaf of bread he'd been shelving. Realizing who it was, his voice shook. "Bradley? What are you doing?"

"I know what you are, Carl," the man growled, re-tightening his grip on the machete. "You're a sympathizer. We can't have people like you running around at night, doing whatever the hell you want."

Without hesitation, Zahra stepped forward. "Okay, let's just think about this. Violence will just land you in jail."

Eden balked. What was Zahra doing? She'd always sought justice, but was talking to a madman the smartest move?

The man called Bradley glared at Zahra. "I'll. Do. Whatever. I. Have. To," he said, repeating every word slower than the last.

The look he gave Zahra was alarming. Threatening. Eden reached for her friend protectively, but Zahra moved too quickly to grab. She stood in front of Carl; fists clenched at her sides.

Carl didn't do anything to sway Zahra to move. He stood behind her comfortably, as he bit back at Bradley. "I don't know what you're talking about. I'm a compliant citizen like the rest of New York."

Bradley didn't say anything. Instead, he sniffed loudly with a quick nod. Then, he galloped across the room with his arm raised. Eden had no time to think before Bradley's blade was moments from hitting both Zahra and Carl.

Like a bolt of lightning, something within crackled from her chest. It spread across her torso, reaching around the ache in her back. Her eyes burned with tears as she watched the man pull his arm back, ready to strike a blow against an innocent girl. Against her best friend.

"Stop!" she screamed, her arm lifting.

The man halted unexpectedly. He turned his head to Eden, his confused eyes deepening with anger. His hand shook as he fought to hold on to the machete.

Eden raised her other arm and flung it in front of her. Her elbows locked, palms out, fingers spread, knuckles white.

The machete flew from the man's hand, spearing the beverage fridge beside him.

"Demon," the man croaked in a frightened whisper. And then louder, "DEMON!"

The word pulsated through Eden's core, but she rejected it. She wasn't a demon, surely. As his dark eyes glared at her in disgust, she felt a trickle of electricity soar through her veins.

"You're the demon," she hissed.

Eden thrust her hands again and a surge of power sent him flying backward, crashing through the glass fridge door. He landed amongst milk and juice and soda, surrounded by shards of glass. Liquid flowed from smashed bottles like the blood that flowed from his broken skin.

There was a moment of silence. No one moved. No one breathed. The instincts that propelled Eden, faded as quickly as they came. Eden twisted her shaking hands and stared at her palms. She wanted to ask if it was her that did that, but she knew it was. As clear as her heart beating against her chest, she knew she had done that.

Lowering her arms, she swallowed and looked to Zahra and Carl. "Are... are you... " she stuttered. "Are you both all right?"

A little shaky, Carl shuffled to his till and bent down to grab a dustpan and brush. Straightening, he wagged it at both of the girls. "You'd better get out of here."

Eden glanced at Bradley, moaning in pain. "But I —"

"Come on," Zahra hushed, clutching Eden's wrist. "We gotta get you outta here."

Zahra hauled a stupefied Eden out of the store. They didn't say a word as she pulled her down the street, a straight line to their apartment building. Only after they'd burst through the doors, and made it safely into the elevator, did Zahra face Eden.

"This changes everything," she cried, steadying a swaying Eden. "I hope you're ready."

Eden

Eden's world felt like it was ending for a long time. Half a life's worth of memories and a blank void to fill the rest. Minuscule gaps of light, hope, *his* eyes.

But this was something else. She stood against the just slammed door of her apartment, lungs filling and deflating too fast. This was more than a memory; this was who she was. Her essence. Her person.

"Rocky Road come at me." Alistair marched down the hall, carrying three bowls and spoons, ready for the goodies Eden was meant to return with.

Eden looked at her empty hands, then ripped the beanie off her head and threw it against Alistair's chest. "Tell me what I need to know."

She huffed past him into the living room and slumped into her chair. Lacey glanced up from her book and a knowing look flitted across her face. "What happened?"

Eden shook her head. "It's my turn to ask the questions."

Lacey placed her book on her lap as Alistair descended into his leather chair, bowls and beanie still in his grasp. He swallowed hard. "Did you follow my rules, Eden?"

"I said, it's my turn to ask the questions." Eden felt her nostrils flare. She closed her eyes briefly to resettle herself but all that did was show her *his* face and those bloodshot eyes. She forced her eyes open. "I need to know. What am I? Who am I? You're waiting for me to remember, but you already know don't you?"

Alistair winced, wrinkles forming on his forehead. Then, he nodded and rested the contents of his hands onto the coffee table. He curled his palms around the armrests of his chair and pushed himself up. He paused, mid-stand, to glance at his wife.

She gave him a demure smile and nodded. "It's the right thing."

Standing, he turned to Eden. "Give me one moment, my sweet. I think you're ready to know the truth of your past."

Mixed emotions swirling, Eden shivered as he walked past her. They'd always known more than she had, she knew that much. But as she listened to her dad unlock his office door, a sudden rush of resentment filled her. How much did they know? And why wait to tell her now?

She turned her palms upward and stared at the lines running across them. Her warm breath rushed through her fingers.

"Eden?" Lacey asked, almost a whisper. She leaped from her chair and knelt before her daughter. She took Eden's hands and squeezed them tight. "Did you remember more?"

Looking into her mother's tear-filled eyes, Eden's breath hitched. She savored these times when Lacey looked at her with a not-so-cold gaze. "I... I think so."

Alistair returned to the living room with nothing in his hands. Eden couldn't remember hearing him close the study door. Normally, the sound of the dramatic slam echoed through the apartment. He took a place next to Lacey. "What did you remember?"

"It wasn't a... It wasn't my mind that remembered something..." Eden stopped. How could she explain it? But, looking between her parents, somehow she knew that they would understand. "It was my body. It remembered how to do something."

With a voice as low as a heartbeat, Alistair asked, "What did it remember to do?"

Thinking about that man, Bradley—his body cut by shattered glass, his blood dripping to the floor, Eden cringed. Surely, she didn't do that. Surely, she didn't throw a man across a room with only a thought. How was it even possible? She licked her lips and shook her head. "Magic?" With her next breath, she rushed out a quick, "What am I?"

Alistair swallowed and rolled back onto his feet. As he stood, he stroked his fingers through Eden's white streak. "You're special."

"Father?" A male voice said from behind them.

Eden jumped to her feet. Startled, she readied her hands, fingers spread wide. Not wanting a repeat of what she'd done at the store, Eden locked her elbows flat against her waist.

Standing in the living room archway was a boy... no, a man. He was tall and muscular and wore nothing but pajama pants made out of muslin. His arms hung by his sides, fingertips nervously tapping onto his thighs.

Alistair rushed to the boy's side and placed a hand on his curved shoulder. "No, we spoke about this. I'm not your father." He smiled sadly then pointed at Eden. "Do you know who this is?"

The boy let his gaze follow Alistair's pointed finger. He cast his eyes on Eden and his crinkled brow rose. The edges of his lips lifted as he said, "I'm not sure. I think so."

Eden's pounding heartbeat thumped against her chest. She clutched the back of her chair as she hunched over. Light's fired across her brain.

"Eden?" Alistair prompted. "Do you know who this is?"

The memory hit without warning. She was in a boat on Lake Louise, her hand dipping through the water as she floated on the calm. She was laughing, happiness bubbling through her body. She peered over her shoulder at the smile beaming back at her— and it was *him.*

His eyes matched the lake.

Back then, his hair was brown with streaks of silver throughout, just like hers.

She returned to the present moment, six whole years later. The name rolled off her tongue. "Kai... Malakai."

"Mal-a-kai," the boy repeated, as though trying it on for size. He turned to Alistair. "Yes, that's right. That's my name."

Eden stepped around her chair, closer to the half-naked boy in front of her. She couldn't take her eyes off him. He was connected to that memory... connected to her.

Something was off though. His hair was completely dark, all brown, no silver. Eden didn't know whether to laugh or cry. "Why did you do this, Dad?"

"I thought he would help you with your memories."

Eden frowned. She let her eyes wander down the divots in his muscular torso and up again. On the front of his left shoulder was a raised scar about the width of a golf ball, light purple in color. In the back of her mind, Eden felt that was significant. She stepped closer and let her hand press against his chest. A steady beat tickled her palm.

He seemed so real.

"Great craftsmanship."

Alistair frowned. "What do you mean?"

Eden took the boy's face in her hands, turning his face side to side in study. A strong jawline complemented his full lips. "He's exactly how I imagined him to look now. Except, he's grown into his chin."

"Umm..." The boy's eyes suddenly became a little brighter. He whispered, "Can you stop touching me, Edie?"

No one called her that. But hearing it sounded familiar, like a cloud-covered full moon. Almost perfect but not quite clear.

"You do know her?" Alistair asked again.

Without moving his eyes from her, Kai replied with a smile, "Yes. It's just come to me. Hello, Eden."

Pursing her lips, Eden stepped back and turned to her mom. "You approved this? It's a little weird, isn't it? What am I supposed to do with..." she let her eyes trace the shape of his body once more. "A robot?"

Kai balked and spun to face Alistair. "I'm a robot?"

"Heavens no," Alistair spat. "Girl, wake up."

Eden shook her head, refusing to believe it. This couldn't be him; it couldn't be the boy who haunted her dreams. Because that boy... he was dead.

Lacey placed her hand on Eden's back as she walked to Kai. "Hello, Malakai, I'm Lacey. Can you tell me how you know Eden?"

Kai squinted as he looked at Eden, his aqua eyes shining even through slits. "We're friends."

"And how are you friends, do you have memories of her?" Alistair pressed.

Kai's lips fell into a pout, his eyebrows lowering. "I don't... she and I, we... we got separated, and she was taken from me. That's..." Kai scanned the room as if searching for the memory right there in the apartment. "That's all I can remember."

"Incredible," Lacey marveled, looking between Kai and Alistair. "It worked. Eden took forever to remember anything and here he is within days."

Eden moved back, her hands finding the top of her chair. Her mind spun, unable to catch up with what was happening around her. She became lost—somewhere between the things this boy was saying and the fact that her parents welcomed him like a long lost puppy.

And then, a sharp yet quiet beep rang out. And another. Over and over an unusual alarm swept through the house.

Welcoming the distraction, Eden ran into the hallway. The study door was wide open, and the repetitive noise seemed to come from inside.

"Eden? Hold up." Alistair called from the living room archway.

But her curiosity had already piqued. She moved closer, her hand resting on the doorframe she'd hardly been allowed to step through. The room was dark and decorated like any normal office. Books filled the floor-to-ceiling shelves. A large timber desk sat in front of the back wall. One thing was different though. A stairwell, once hidden, led up from an opening in the bookshelf. Eden stopped and stared as yet another beep rang long and loud.

Lacey brushed past Eden and bolted into the office. She tapped furiously at the top of the desk. In response, one side of the desk raised and a secret compartment popped out. She lifted a tablet from within as another beep resonated from it. As soon as Lacey swiped the tablet, the noise ceased.

It wasn't a normal night from the beginning. After a normal interrogation, Lacey would either read or bake, but there she was pulling out a device Eden had only seen in movies, using it as though it was the most natural thing in the world. Eden glanced to Alistair then back to Lacey, suddenly looking at her parents with new eyes. They'd never been normal, but this was different. They knew things. And Eden couldn't help wonder what people she'd been living with all these years.

Lacey looked up then, eyes widening at Eden. She shouted, "Alistair! They've found her."

Alistair stormed into the study and peered at the tablet over Lacey's shoulder. He breathed in sharply, hands raking through his hair. Peering at Eden, he whimpered, "But she's not ready."

Behind Eden, a creak in the floorboard made her spin. She raised her arm, palm pointed out, energy buzzing beneath the surface.

The half-naked boy blinked slowly, his hands raising in surrender. "It's just me. Kai. Remember?"

Eden's heart pounded hard against her ribs. Everything was moving too fast. Still looking at Kai, she asked her parents, "What do I need to be ready for?"

Lacey stepped in front of Eden. "You used your powers, didn't you?"

Eden swallowed. All this time they were asking her what she could remember when she should have been the one asking them. Defiantly, she lifted her chin. "What powers?"

Lacey shook her head and peered down to the tablet. "There's no time to explain. They're already on the second floor."

Eden stole a glance. A blueprint of their whole apartment building lit up the tablet screen. Little red dots were circling the stairs. Lacey double tapped the screen to show the third floor, then again for the fourth. Moving her eyes to her mother's distraught face, Eden stepped back.

Alistair grabbed a hold of Eden's shoulder, shaking her back to reality. "He's still working through his memories. You need to protect him."

Eden guffawed. "Me? Protect him? You're kidding."

"Wake up, girl." Alistair squeezed her shoulders tighter and motioned his head at his office. "Look around you. We've played happy families for long enough."

"I'm awake," Eden said, staring at the staircase in his study. She'd never seen it on any of the occasions he'd let her in there. Not that there were many occasions. "I'm wide awake. Trust me."

She knew they weren't a normal family. Most of the time she chose to ignore it. But that night, right then, it was so close in her face she couldn't escape it.

"Anyway"—she threw an arm in Kai's direction, gesturing to his muscles—"I don't see how I can protect him. He looks like he should be protecting me."

Kai covered his chest with his arms and shivered. He looked so innocent, so hopeless, so confused. Eden frowned, feeling a little guilty for her outburst. Maybe he really did need to be protected. But from what?

"Yes, both ways," Lacey said, rushing back into the office. "Now hurry, because they're coming!"

Alistair rushed in behind her. Within seconds they ran out with a shotgun each.

"My God!" Eden groaned. "Who are you people?"

Lacey jerked the gun toward the front door and looked over her shoulder. Through gritted teeth, she hissed, "Get out of here, the two of you."

"Here." Alistair tapped the watch hugging Eden's wrist. To her surprise, a holographic screen popped up, displaying exactly what the tablet had. He pointed to the red dots filing from the stairwell onto the seventh floor. "They are bad. Stay away from them."

Eden gawked at the surveillance and watched five red dots running in a straight line to their apartment. More secrets crawled out of the cracks. All the times he'd made her wear that watch, and she never knew it could do that.

"Eden!" Alistair yelled, grabbing her chin and forcing her to look at him. "Go."

Eden blinked, shaking herself out of her shock. She double tapped the watch, and the projector vanished. She turned to Kai. "Can he have clothes on at least?"

Kai

He knew her. The feeling came before the memory. Of friendship, camaraderie, an unbreakable bond. Yes, he knew her. He didn't quite know why but being near her now was all that mattered.

She stood beside him dumbfounded, staring at her parents as though they were strangers. They had told them to run and he couldn't quite comprehend why she wasn't doing just that. Kai wanted to shake her out of it, something in him wanted to respond—to save her. But still he didn't touch Eden, because, despite these instincts, he didn't want to upset her.

One hard thump against the door and it burst open.

In the doorway, stood three burly men dressed in black. They swayed as though they were mere shadows; men, yet not, like all life had left their eyes.

Alistair fired the first shot.

The bullet whizzed through the air and Kai jolted. He grabbed Eden by the hand and pulled her away from the gunfire. As he dragged her toward the kitchen, she resisted the whole way, twisting to see her parents.

Another shot rang out and a grumbling, not-quite-human, noise echoed down the hallway. Eden gasped, still trying to pry her hand from Kai's grasp. He looked over his shoulder to see Lacey throw the butt of her gun across the face of one man. He caught a glimpse of the man's face—wrinkled, yet he didn't move like he was old. The man fell to the ground and bounced right up to his feet again. Without hesitation, he used the butt of his own gun to smack the back of Lacey's head. A slight whimper and she collapsed in a heap. When Lacey remained motionless for too long, Kai's grip tightened on Eden.

"Nooo!" Eden cried, planting her feet to pull against him. "Let me go!"

The man that hovered over Lacey jerked his head, and, as his obsidian eyes found Eden, Kai yanked her into the kitchen.

Something about those men's faces, their movements... it frightened him. Kai didn't know them, not truly, but seeing them sparked something inside his mind. He'd been hazy since he woke up from what felt like a lifetime of dreaming. He couldn't quite shake off the foggy moment between being asleep and awake. But right then, in that moment of panic, something clicked. Something small, but something nonetheless.

In his distraction, Eden yanked her hand out of his grasp. As she pulled away, the man with obsidian eyes entered the kitchen. Out of pure instinct, Kai stepped in front of Eden.

The man flinched, staring at Kai in what could have been mistaken for fear. A sense of knowing filled Kai's senses and a tiny smirk lit his face. This not-quite-human was afraid of him. Confidently, Kai rolled his shoulders and steadied his stance in front of Eden.

This close, Kai could see that what first appeared

to be wrinkles, were in fact scars lining the curves of his face. Black blood ran through the veins along his neck, reaching for his chin.

With shaking hands, the man raised his gun, aiming directly at Kai's chest.

The sound of gunfire was paired with Eden's scream. She lunged around Kai, arm out and palm facing the man. As if by magic, the bullet stopped inches from Kai's chest. It levitated in the air for a moment, before floating backward. At first, the progress was slow, like his mind was replaying his last moment in reverse. But then Eden threw her other arm forward and the bullet shot with lightning speed back from where it came from. It hit the man's shoulder, crunching loudly as it tore through bone.

"Bitch!" the man hissed as he clutched the wound and retreated down the hall.

It wasn't the word he'd used or even the tone of his voice; it was the threatening glare the man gave Eden that was enough to raise an almighty stir within Kai. Eden didn't need protecting, in fact, she just protected him. Regardless, his fists balled and he jumped into the hallway in time to watch the man run out of the apartment, dodging Lacey's body as he went.

Another man watched him leave with disdain before moving to Lacey, gun pointed at her still breathing chest. Eden was quick to join Kai, and he swore he heard the smallest of moans expel at the sight of her mother. The sound of her internal agony sent his heart into overdrive.

"Hey!" Eden called. "You want us? Come get us."

Kai spun to her. "What are you doing?"

She winced at the question but didn't respond. Her chin raised as a man came from the living room, joined by another in the hallway. As the two of them marched forward, Kai thought about wrapping his arms around Eden's torso and running away. But the men blocked their escape.

Alistair stumbled under the archway, blood pouring from his nose. He wiped it once and croaked, "For Heaven's sake, girl. Get out of here."

This time, it was Eden who grabbed Kai's hand. She led him through the kitchen to the fire escape, moving slow enough to make sure the men followed, but also quick enough to keep distance. She ripped the window open and pointed wildly outside.

Kai almost chuckled at her cute desperation but the sound of two men barreling into the kitchen was enough to obey her orders. He climbed through the window and stood on a grated balcony.

Night had fallen, drones and stars lit the sky. Crisp air sent shivers along his torso. He crossed his arms, peering down the seven floors to the barren world below.

Eden slammed the window behind her and pushed him against the wall out of sight, taking a second to look down then up. The top floor was only three flights, compared to the seven to the ground. In a split second, it seemed she made her choice. "Come on."

As she began climbing the ladder to the roof, the window creaked open. Kai rushed to follow her, his foot barely touching the first rung as one of the men poked his head through the window.

The same protective instinct from before surged through his body.

There were many things Kai was unsure of. Did he have a home? Did he have a family? Was he possibly a robot like Eden thought? He didn't know what a gun was or that being out at night was illegal. What he did know was this: Eden was important to him and he could tear limbs from these men if he wanted to. Literally.

He moved without thought as his foot collided hard with the man's face. Blood splattered as he cried out, clutching his nose. Kai looked on with a smirk.

The man shook his head, as blood glistened over

his lips, he returned the smile to Kai and stepped through the window.

"Hurry!" Eden called, pulling herself up.

Kai swallowed, her voice inflaming the stir already swirling inside him. As the man rushed forward, Kai jumped off the ladder onto the landing and flung his arm out. His hand immediately connecting with the man's chest, Kai's fingers gripped the shirt. He took a moment to admire the sturdy material as it bunched against his palm. He smirked again, biceps rippling as he lifted the man off the ground.

"I'm sorry, I'm sorry. I'm just obeying orders," the man begged, arms flailing.

Kai's gaze flitted to the second man clambering out of the apartment before returning his glare to the first. Without strain, Kai lowered the man's face nearer to his. Words he didn't know the meaning of growled out of his mouth, "You chose this."

Then, as though he was tossing a feather, he threw the man into the other and they both went crashing into the kitchen. Kai slammed the window shut behind them and returned to the ladder.

Climbing with grace and speed, he caught up to Eden on the ninth floor landing within seconds. For a moment, he wasn't quite sure whether she had stopped climbing or if he really was that quick.

"How did you—" she began.

Adrenaline pumping, he streamlined past her and flung himself over the top rail onto the roof.

The air was stale with city smog. There wasn't much difference between daytime and nighttime, except for the darkness that shrouded the buildings. It was quiet too, aside from the sound of Eden still clambering up the fire escape.

Kai spun around, his brain ticking. It was a weird feeling for him. Like lightning inside a cluster of fog. He didn't know who he was or where he was from, but he instinctively knew Eden, and the protectiveness that came with it was overwhelming. It ruled him.

Eden threw herself onto the roof and checked to make sure no one was following. She moved away from the edge and sighed. "They've gone."

Visibly relaxing, she strolled across the roof past a set of lounge chairs. Three to be exact. Kai watched her as her fingers danced along the tops of them, her face turning upward to the darkened sky.

"I've never been out past curfew," Eden said thoughtfully. She glanced at Kai, her eyes falling up and down his half-naked body. "We should go back to see if my parents are okay."

"Should we? Didn't they tell us to leave?" Kai asked.

Eden's face changed. Pain evident. She took a long breath, in and then out. "I can't just leave them; did you see my mother?"

A drone buzzed down the street, lights shining in a circular motion as it went. Eden froze, eyes wide.

5

Kai

A hint of the girl Eden used to be flashed through Kai's mind. The memory didn't take long to follow. She was older now than the last time he'd seen her. Back then, when they were separated by a glass wall, he'd never felt so much pain. Those eyes, he could never forget those eyes—tear-filled and broken. At least her tears had dried but looking into her pale blue irises, he could still feel the pain that remained.

"What are those things?" Kai said a little too loudly.

"Shush," Eden hushed. "If it sees us, we're toast."

On the other side of the roof, clothes and sheets flapped in the breeze. Eden ran to a line and hastily ripped a black T-shirt free. She threw it at Kai.

"Get dressed," she hissed, hurrying on the pads of her feet toward a small conservatory at the back corner of the roof.

Pulling the T-shirt over his head, Kai tiptoed behind her and entered the glass dome. Inside, three rows of plants and blooming flowers filled the tight space. Warmth hit him first, and then the smell—a sweet and earthy scent that seemed like it would cling to his aura if he stayed there long enough. He walked down a row, marveling at a giant yellow flower.

Eden closed the door. "You act like you've never seen a sunflower before."

"Sunflower," Kai repeated, stroking a petal between two fingers.

The drone moved along the side of the apartment block, light hitting the part of the roof where they'd stood moments earlier. Eden rushed to Kai and crouched down, pulling him to the ground with her.

"Don't move. Don't speak. Don't breathe," she whispered.

Lights circled the conservatory, hitting green leaves and ripened tomatoes before moving on. Eden sighed, and Kai smiled at the sight of her relief. "Drones, bad. Sunflowers, good?"

Calm washed from Eden's face and her eyes turned into slits. He felt her stare rip through his soul. She was not pleased and somehow Kai felt like it was all his fault. Maybe it was.

"Those men, bad. My parents, good." She stood up decisively. "I'm going back for them."

Kai didn't think it was a great idea. Those oafs were probably still in the apartment. But her expression gave him pause, how could he say no to that face? Besides, he was strong, really strong. He threw that man on the balcony without breaking a sweat.

Nodding, he said, "Okay."

But something changed in the time it took him to stand. He cocked his head, his gaze focusing to the space behind Eden. Without another second passing, he reached for her, pulling her body against him.

A look of disgust fell across her face and she writhed out of his hold. With Kai too focused on the danger behind her, she slipped too easily from him.

Then, the glass door swung open.

"Look out," Kai yelled, reaching for her again.

He wasn't quick enough, though. The man Eden had magically shot rushed into the conservatory and lunged for her. Her eyes widened as he tackled her to the ground with a thud. Her head cracked against the cold cement.

A line of crimson trickled through her brown hair. The sight of Eden pinned under this creature, struggling for breath as he crushed her with his weight, made Kai's blood run cold. Rage fueling him, he lurched forward.

He slammed his hand around the back of the man's neck, squeezing his fingers hard against the flesh. With only one hand, he lifted the monster off Eden. A low guttural moan rumbled from Kai's throat as he stormed out of the conservatory and threw the man. As if he were a rag doll, the body tumbled through the air. It cleared the edge of the building and skidded across the roof of the next.

Kai waited with anticipation for any sign of life. An elbow jerked as the man struggled to rise, falling back down with shaking limbs. A hint of disappointment laced Kai's voice as he turned around and grumbled, "Don't these things ever die?"

Eden leaned against the doorway of the conservatory, gasping for air. She clasped the frame and stepped out, knees knocking. Her eyes flicked to the fire escape in silent alarm.

It was enough to alert Kai. He spun around in time to see the other two men breach the roof. By the time he realized they had guns, it was too late. Pain blossomed across his body as the bullets buried themselves into his body—one in his thigh, another in his stomach, and one right where his heart was.

Behind him, Eden's scream echoed through the night. Warm blood poured; deep pain followed. Was this how it was always going to end? With half a memory and a hint of something meaningful? Were his God-given powers all for nothing?

His knees buckled beneath him. But as his body thought about giving up, something took a hold of him. An invisible strength held him upright.

And then, he was flying. Backward. As though pulled by thin air. For a moment, he wondered if he was dying, being dragged into hell.

Back he went, heels barely touching the ground. He looked at the men, still pointing their guns with wide, dark eyes. Their fingers squeezed the triggers and more bullets pierced his chest, nestling themselves into fatal crevices.

Soon, he was back inside the conservatory and Eden's shaking hands found his back as she lowered him to the ground. She looked as lost as he felt.

"Did you bring me back here, Edie?" It hurt him to speak.

Her eyes were like saucers as she studied his wounds. "Oh my God." She gasped. "Oh my God," she repeated, pressing her hands onto the places where blood rushed. "Oh, God."

"God can't help you down here," a man rasped.

Eden jumped up and turned around, facing the two men as they breached the conservatory. Both of them raised their guns once more. Kai felt Eden's heels against his leg as she inched back. He strained himself to sit up.

"Please," Eden begged. "You've already shot him enough to kill him. What more do you want?"

The first man cocked his head and eyed his companion, who nodded in reply. He lowered his gun and dug his hand into a pocket, retrieving a bronze clasp that glowed like the moon. The man wagged it at Eden. "Come gently."

A flash of a memory whipped through Kai's mind. The clasp around his wrist, around Eden's wrist.

Agony followed.

"No!" Kai demanded, finding his voice. He rose to his knees, puffing, holding whichever bullet wound hurt the most.

Both men aimed their weapons, one at Eden and one at Kai. As their fingers began pressing the trigger, Eden groaned. She raised an arm and flicked her wrist up. The two men careened to the glass ceiling, stuck as if suspended by ropes.

Beyond the glass dome, Kai heard the sound of a nearby drone. As he stood, he caught sight of the drone hovering above the roof of the apartment, flashing its spotlight on the still moaning body. It began searching around the body for more movement, its radius getting larger with every millisecond.

"I told you those guns were useless," one man said, his face smooshed against the glass ceiling.

Eden turned to face Kai, her outstretched arms shaking. She glanced up and down his body. "You're okay?"

He looked down at his chest, surprised that the pain he'd just felt had all but disappeared. There was blood but no wounds, not even scars. He took a deep breath and clenched his fists, ready for war.

"Quick," Eden urged. "Go find help. I don't know how long I can hold them."

Out of the corner of his eye, Kai saw the drone move closer. He gave a sad smile and reached, wrapping his gentle fingers around her wrist. Touching her smooth skin made his breath hasten. He lowered his head and whispered, "Not without you, Edie."

Her gray eyes softened. It was almost as though she recognized him the way that he knew her. But the moment was fleeting.

"You two think you're so special, don't you?" one man garbled.

"Don't worry," the other one said. "They don't know

who they are. Just look at them. Confused little kids, haunted by memories they don't have."

Eden tore her eyes from Kai, staring at them with a piercing glare. "What do you know about our memory loss?"

The first man flinched and hushed his companion. "Shut up, dude. You know what she's capable of, don't push her buttons."

"Oh, who am I to care? In a day or two they'll both be comatose again. This will all be a darkened blip hidden in their brains."

The way they talked to each other seemed strange to Kai. They weren't just callous; they spoke as if they had no souls. The tone of their voices sent shivers down his spine.

"Enough!" Eden screamed. "What do you know? Tell me what you know."

A maniacal guffaw danced off the glass and echoed around the dome. "Oh, sweet little innocence. Child, don't you know? Your life is meaningless. Your memories don't matter. You're just a payday."

Kai could feel the anger explode out of Eden like an atom bursting. She flung her arm wide, sending the bodies dragging through the glass ceiling from one end to the other. The moment she relaxed, two bodies crashed to the ground. The sound of bones breaking echoed around the dome.

Kai slowly turned. Two men lay sprawled along the tomatoes and sunflowers. Arms and legs twisted into places they shouldn't be. One man lay on his stomach, a pool of blood seeping around his head.

The other, half under the first, eyes wide open, bone sticking out of his shoulder. Red blood, yes, but also black. Darkened and glistening like ore. His open eyes were black, not just the iris, the whole of it. Scars lined his face, not purple or red like most, gray and deep—like he wasn't quite human. Claw-like fingernails stuck out at the ends of both their hands.

Eden gasped, a sudden realization of what she'd just done. She stared at her palms. "Did I do that?"

Protectiveness overtook his movements. Kai blocked her view from the mess and let his hand fall into hers. He tugged on her to turn around, and as he began walking backward across the roof, he whispered, "Keep your eyes on me, Edie."

She followed him, legs weakening underneath her with every step. Despite Kai's warning, she looked over her shoulder. For a moment, she was frozen, staring at the deceased.

A drone whooshed by, fixing its light on the scene. Another soon joined. In the distance, more began zooming in their direction.

Footsteps echoed up through the internal stairwell. Kai looked for the man he threw over to the next building, but he was gone. He let his ears strain as the footsteps grew louder, closer.

"Edie?" Kai asked, tugging gently on her hand to follow. "We have to leave."

Eden nodded. And silently, they climbed down the fire escape, moving faster with every landing.

6

Eden

On the edge of the East River, underneath the Brooklyn Bridge, two scared teenagers huddled on the pillars. New York used to be called the city that never sleeps. That was before a time Eden could remember though. Outside was only ever meant for daytime.

The lights of fast-moving drones reflected off the water. Eden could count seven along the river alone. More hovered above the buildings, along the roads, down the boardwalk to Jane's carousel. They were searching for any sign of life.

She lifted her wrist and pushed the buttons on the watch like her father showed her. A screen popped out of the watch face, a blueprint of the whole city. White lines showed buildings and something new, she looked at a drone across the river, weaving down the pathway beside the river's edge. On the screen, the same drone was white, a flashing light. White dots peppered the map, the whole city under constant surveillance.

On the east side of the map, farther into Midtown Manhattan, a small cluster of blue dots shone. A red dot moved south, fast away from her home, a few blocks away.

Eden often wondered what lurked in the dark. Rumors of demons were whispered on street corners and blasted over the news. She'd never seen one though, at least not until tonight.

"I don't remember much about... well, anything. But I know those men were not normal men." Kai rubbed at his shoulder blades.

Eden wiped her cheek, wet from tears. Another one replaced it immediately. She buried her face into her hands and her back slid down the cold cement of the pillar. When her backside hit the ground, she looked up to the sky. Cloud and smog joined together but a few stars shined through, framed by the skyline.

She watched the clouds pass over, mesmerized by the evening sky. Something she'd only seen through glass or as a picture. Whenever she felt alone or different, which was often, she'd rip her drapes apart and stare up into the night sky. Its vastness gave her peace. Nostalgia from a time gone by, a time she could feel but couldn't remember. It made her feel like home; like she was whole. Even though she was missing pieces that were scattered as far and wide as the stars across the night sky.

"You know, I always had this silly notion that they could be spies. But now I know it's something worse. They used to be scientists before I came along. They gave it up to be a family but I know that's not true. They gave it up to protect something." Eden paused, trying not to think about the powers she'd suddenly acquired, and trying even harder not to replay the blood that was spilled because of her inability to control it. "They were hiding something... me."

With eyes still scanning the sky above, she rested her head back onto the pillar. Kai stood beside her. Feeling his gaze, she glanced at him. "Shit. I'm talking to a robot."

Kai didn't respond to her comment. Instead, he let himself collapse beside her. "Should we go back to save them?"

Eden gave Kai her full attention then. She sighed. "A robot with empathy. Just what I need."

"Robots don't have emotions or memories. Besides, if I'm a robot, what are you? I saw what you did to those men." Kai lifted his knees and flung his arms over them. Playing with something between his fingers.

Frowning, Eden lifted her own hands and stared. Robots don't have memories? Maybe she was a robot, too? That's why all the secrecy with her parents. That's why she couldn't remember anything before she was twelve.

But then, what were the memories of *him?* She moved her gaze to his twitching hands and noticed a cigarette butt pressed in his fingertips. She lurched forward and flicked the butt away. It flew across in front of them and ricocheted off a pillar of the fence before splashing into the water.

"What are you doing?" she snapped.

Kai placed his arms across his chest. "What?"

"You don't just pick up rubbish..." She stopped when his aqua eyes hooded. He didn't know what it was. Just like he didn't know what a drone or a sunflower was. "How much do you remember?"

"I woke up two days ago. So... two days, plus little snippets from before."

Eden frowned. It had taken her six months to learn how to even talk. She looked at the bullet holes in his top and imagined the shape of the scar on his shoulder. How could he have a scar if he could heal? Yes, he was definitely a robot.

"I also remember your eyes," he added.

She frowned again, feeling his eyes bore into her. Avoiding his stare, she looked back up to the sky. A drone flew over, its searchlight circling the bridge above them. Eden held her breath until it moved on.

"Wide like a deer's," Kai continued, still looking at her.

Closing her eyes, Eden huffed. "How do you know what a deer is?"

He was silent for a moment before saying, "I just do."

Eden brought her gaze down, locking onto his blue eyes. They were so fierce, so earnest. His stare felt like truth, threatening to shine light throughout her core, bringing everything hidden to light. Her heart thumped twice against her rib cage. Hard. She winced at the feeling he gave her. "Let me get this straight," she said, shuffling herself away a bit. "You don't know what a cigarette is, but you know what a deer is?"

Kai nodded once. "And you, I know what you are... who you are... and your deer-like eyes."

"Anyway, the saying isn't deer-like eyes, it's doe eyes."

"Okay... You have doe eyes. And the memory of them, a younger version, makes me smile."

Somehow she was looking at him again. She bit her lip, subconsciously reprimanding herself. She didn't want to tell him how the memory of his pained and blood-shot eyes made her feel sick.

Eden shook her head and rose to her feet. She reminded herself they weren't *his* eyes. They weren't the real Kai's eyes. Not this cheap knock-off.

A drone buzzed close. It was lower than the others as it swept above the river. It swooped under the bridge and stopped at the fence in front of them, light scanning up and down. It hit the water and stopped at the cigarette butt a little longer than normal. Eden froze. She'd never broken curfew before. Never tempted the authority. She didn't even know what would happen if she got caught. What it would do, where it would take her.

The drone's light lifted back to the fence, right

where the cigarette butt hit before it fell. And, as if tracing its flight backward, the drone's light arched across and rested on Kai's fingers.

The drone paused, made a shudder, then started beeping. In the distance, identical beeps began rushing toward them. Echoing off walls and wet pavement, charging down the river. All pathways to the bridge. All headed for them.

"Shoosh," Eden hushed, in an attempt to stop it.

The drone's light quickly flashed from Kai's hands to Eden's face. The beeping noise suddenly double-timed. Louder and in faster succession. Kai darted his head up at Eden, eyes widening with fear.

Without another moment's hesitation, he grabbed the drone in his hand and slammed it down on the ground. It was in pieces before another beep could sound. The distant sound of rushing drones ceased. The collection of them soaring above the river, breaking apart and searching back on track.

Kai dusted himself off and stood, too. "Something else I know?" he said, leaning down with a whisper. "We probably should find better shelter until morning."

Eden looked around the area, making sure no drones were too close nearby. She lifted her wrist and tapped the watch. The screen popped up and Eden tapped at the image until she found her apartment building. Not a single red dot in the neighborhood.

She snapped the projector off and said. "We're going home."

7

Eden

The front door was wide open. Eden traced her fingers over the bullet hole in the frame her father had made when the demon-men broke in. Eden stepped inside, her eyes finding the spot where her mother had lain. The hallway was bare though, bar the broken tablet shattered on the ground.

"Mom? Dad?" Eden called walking into the living room. The sign of struggle was still present. Her patchwork chair laid on its side and her mother's favorite books were scattered across the floor. Drawers had been opened and emptied; nothing was left untouched.

Kai closed the door and joined her in the living room. "I don't think they're here."

Eden sighed. It's not like she expected her parents to be home. She knew they'd either escaped or had been captured. She hoped with her whole being it was the former. And hope was all she had in that moment.

She lifted her wrist and tapped at the watch. A bird's-eye view of the apartment appeared. In the living room, two faint blue dots pulsated at their exact location.

Eden made a full circle, exclaiming, "Something's here!"

Kai rushed to her side and peered down at the screen. Seeing the dots, he pulled her down and crawled behind the upturned chair. Together, they hid, crouching with held breaths.

A moment of silence passed. Eden lifted the watch and zoomed in on the dots. She twisted her hand so Kai could see.

He peered over the chair, eyes darting around the room. "We know you're there!" he shouted. "You may as well come out."

Another moment passed. Nothing but beating hearts and hastened exhales.

"Wait here," Kai whispered before standing. He began creeping across the room to the hallway.

Eden gawked at the projection, watching one of the dots move. "Oh my God... It's us."

"What?" Kai asked, turning around.

"The dots..." Eden stood and pointed to the watch. "The blue dots are us."

As Kai moved closer to get a better look, so did the dot, back from the hallway and into the living room, stopping next to the other dot.

"Well, it would have been good if he told us that before." Kai sighed, visibly relaxing. "And we're the only ones here?"

Eden zoomed out a little to see the whole apartment, she flicked her finger over the projection and it spun around. She squeezed the blueprint and turned it sideways to get a better look at the whole building. "That's weird."

"What is?" Kai moved closer until their shoulders grazed.

"There aren't any other blue dots, just us," she said, zooming in on the third floor and Zahra's apartment. "There are definitely more people in this block but it's not showing them."

Kai shrugged and stepped away. He picked up Eden's toppled chair. "Maybe it just shows robots."

Eden swung her head over her shoulder and glared. He wasn't looking though; he was busy collecting books from the floor. A small smirk lighting his face.

"Smart-ass," she muttered, turning the projector off. "My point is, we can't see anyone else on this watch. How can we know for sure they aren't here? Or at least hiding in the building? For all we know, they're at our friends' house downstairs right now, wondering what the hell to do?" Her feet twitched under her, ready to run.

Kai placed a pile of books on the edge of the coffee table. He lifted his hands in surrender, almost as if preempting her next move. Cautiously, so as not to upset her, he said, "Edie, think about it. We're being hunted by those... things. I doubt your parents will let innocent people get caught in the cross fire. You think they'd just run to a friend's house and put more people in danger?"

Eden hadn't thought about it like that. It stung a little to be told by someone who didn't know the first thing about anything. She rolled her eyes, too proud to show him the smallest of inklings that he might be right, and too disenchanted to believe that this boy standing in front of her could be the one from her memories. And also, if she had allowed herself to be honest, she was completely and utterly petrified. It was up to her to save her parents but she really had no idea where to even start.

Well, there was somewhere she could start.

Her boots slammed against the floorboards as she marched into her father's study. The same room once off limits was hers for the taking. With no locks to keep her out, she stormed in.

Dark, wooden floor-to-ceiling shelves and the smell of old books slowed her. The room felt calming as soon as she stepped inside. It satisfied her, a knowing that she was in the right place for answers.

She danced her fingertips over the mahogany desk as she marveled at a feather quill, taking pride of place in the middle. She traced the edges of the feather, black at the base and white at the tip. It sent a tingly sensation running up her arm.

"What are you doing?" Kai asked, entering the room.

Eden snapped her hand to a shoulder blade, and dreamily said, "Looking for something."

Her gaze drifted to the stairs made visible by a moved bookshelf. A bright light emanated from above. She charged up, bounding two steps at a time.

The secret room was a little disappointing. It was small, maybe the size of a bathroom, and almost bare. An empty glass cabinet separated the monotony of clinical white walls, and a long steel table sat awkwardly in the middle of the room. Beneath the table, broken vials laid in puddles of blue liquid. In the corner of the room, a smaller steel table held a computer. The screen displayed a message: Backup Failed. She clicked the mouse a few times, but the screen glitched and made a low screeching beep.

"What is this place?" Eden wondered out loud.

"This is where I woke up."

As Eden turned to see Kai touching the long steel table, her foot knocked something. A broken picture frame. She bent down to shake the glass off. As she stood, she stared at the photo. A capture of the three of them from the night they brought her home when she was twelve. One of her earliest memories.

She glared at her parents. For so long she'd wondered who she was and where she was from, but maybe the people she should have been concerned with where those right beside her. She touched the face of her twelve-year-old self, so innocent and confused. Everything had changed since then, but the question still remained. "Who are you?"

"Hey!" Kai said cheerfully, stepping beside her. "That's the Eden I remember."

Eden practically slammed the frame face down onto the table and moved back down the stairs. She went straight for the desk, ignoring the feather this time. She pulled at the handles, but the drawers wouldn't budge. Annoyed, she banged on the top of the desk. What did her mother do to open the compartment?

She bent down to look under the desk, searching for a hidden button or lever. Within a second, Kai dropped to his knees beside her, staring in the same direction she was. When she turned her head to glare at him, he smiled. "What are you looking for?"

Huffing, Eden stood up. She wished he wasn't so damn endearing. It made hating him more effort than she needed. She needed to forget about him, and the memories his face reminded her of. What she needed to do was to find answers. But the more she stayed in that room, the less calm she felt.

The answers were there; they had to be. She hit the desk and yelled, "Open dammit!"

Out of the corner of her eye, she saw Kai looking at her. He stood up, still staring. Then, he turned to the desk. Grabbing it with one hand, he shook. The large heavy wood buckled under the pressure and the compartment popped open.

"Thanks, Robot," Eden said, pulling out the hidden part. Inside was a stash of money rolled into a rubber band and a book. She shoved the money into her pocket and placed the book on the table. She lifted the compartment and turned it upside down. "Is that all?"

"This could be important." Kai flicked through the book.

Eden closely watched the pages as he scoured

through. It was all jumbled. Names and addresses of banks and car detailers and doctors and science labs... she broke away, eyes wandering to the staircase.

"This one's different," Kai said, bringing her attention back to the book.

A name was written in dark blue ink, different from the black of everything else. Her name was scripted in her mother's handwriting, while everything else was her father's scrawl.

"Halfway House. Nancy Withers." Eden read. "Trenton, New Jersey. I've heard them mention her name a few times, but only always in a whisper."

"Halfway house?"

Eden snatched the book from his grasp and nodded. "It's like a place to go for safety, a shelter between two places."

"That sounds promising," Kai replied, but it sounded more like a question than a statement. "Maybe your parents are there, or at least, maybe she knows where your parents are?"

"Maybe..." Eden snapped the book shut and put it back on the desk. "We can't go there anyway. We need a passport to go to New Jersey and..." She looked him up and down. "Robots don't have passports."

His bottom lip curled out. "It'd be great if you stopped calling me a robot, Edie. Anyway, what's a passport?"

"Ugh, of course, you don't know what a passport is." Eden huffed, wandering over to her dad's filing cabinet. "Let's keep looking."

"What are we looking for?" Kai asked, spinning in a circle in the middle of the room.

"Anything that will give us a clue to where my parents are." She opened the cabinet and flicked through. Legal documents. House designs. Mumbo jumbo. Nothing.

"Passport," Kai said behind her.

Eden sighed and looked over her shoulder. "Are we still on that? I told you it—"

With a tiny smirk, Kai held up his hand. In his grasp was a small rectangular booklet. A passport.

"Where did you get that?" Eden said rushing to him. "My passport is kept in the living room desk."

When she reached him she realized it wasn't her passport though.

It was *his*.

Malakai Michaels.

Eden

"We'll go visit her in the morning." Eden wandered down the hallway, marveling at the passport. Her dad must have made it somehow, in preparation. "Hopefully she has some idea about where my parents are."

Eden swiped a blanket from the chest near the entrance of the living room. Next, she scurried into the bathroom, collecting scissors, hair dye, and a hand mirror. Arms full, she headed for the living room.

Kai followed her like a lost puppy. "We can't stay here; those demons know where you live."

Eden dropped the blanket onto the futon and placed the remaining items onto the coffee table. Stepping back, she raised her hand and tapped the button on her dad's watch. Two faint blue dots pulsated in the center. She hit the screen again.

"It will do for tonight," she said, pulling her hair into a low ponytail.

She picked up the scissors and passed them to Kai. He stared at them, confused.

"They're scissors." Eden gawked. "You cut things with them."

Blinking, Kai looked up. "Right. Yeah, I knew that. What do you want me to cut?"

"My hair," Eden said, turning around. "Just under the hair tie. Keep it as straight as you can."

Eden waited a few seconds.

She glanced over her shoulder to find him staring at the scissors, gripping the blades in his palm. Eden carefully placed her fingers around the loops and pried them from him. When the blade was out of his grasp, she sighed. "I would have thought for a robot you'd be hardwired for things like that."

A disdainful look passed across his face. Frowning, he shook his head and moved to the futon. He let his hand brush over the blanket, before sliding under it and lying down. Eden watched him as he meticulously rolled the top of the bedding over and straightened it across his chest.

"You're staring, again," he said, closing his eyes.

"I'm not." Eden huffed. She grabbed the mirror and balanced it against the television. As she plonked herself on the ground in front of it, she cocked her head. "And what do you mean again?"

Kai didn't reply. Eden could see him in the mirror's reflection. He was still lying down with his eyes closed —smirking.

Sighing, she held the scissors and reached around her head. Slowly, she snipped through the locks. Tendrils of brown and white fell to the floor behind her. Eden pulled out the tie. Hair fell around her face, bouncing just above her shoulders. Next, she grabbed the tube of dye and squeezed the contents down her streak. After she'd smoothed it through evenly, she scuttled back to get a better look. It was different, but that was the point. If those creatures were after her, she'd at least make it hard for them to recognize her.

Eden turned to look at Kai, expecting to see him

asleep. She startled to find him sitting up, arms draped over his knees, staring at her. Captivated by his face, she smacked her lips together.

"I remembered something," he said, head tilted. "About you."

"What?" She barely got the word out.

Kai smiled. Not a smirk but a true smile, sincere and encouraging. "We kissed once. It was sweet and innocent, no tongues in case you're wondering."

"We did not!" Eden blurted, startled by her own defense. "I think I'd remember something like that. You made that up, you wouldn't know. You're a robot after all."

"Stop with that already. I'm no more a robot than you are." Kai slumped back onto the futon, throwing an arm in her direction.

Eden turned to face the mirror, but instead of looking at her face she looked at her blue-stained hands. "Maybe I am."

"I remembered something else, too," Kai said.

Eden moaned and faced him. "Listen, we need sleep. If you don't mind we have a big day tomorrow and I'd rather not spend the night listening to your made up memor—"

The sight of Kai rubbing his back jarred her. He winced in pain as he kneaded between his shoulder blades. Knowing what that felt like, Eden softened.

She fell onto her patchwork chair. "Fine. One more."

Kai looked up with a smirk. "Well, I don't know anymore. If you reacted that way to one little kiss I'm not sure you can handle this memory. Maybe you should remember it yourself."

With that he rolled over and closed his eyes, leaving Eden stuck in a feeling between compassion and annoyance.

Glow-in-the-dark stars teased Eden as she lay in her bed. On a rare mother/daughter day, Lacey helped Eden place constellations strategically on the ceiling. At the time, they comforted Eden, giving her a piece of the outside inside. Now though, they reminded her of what she'd lost.

She bunched her quilt up to her neck, making shapes out of the shadows in her room—eyes wide and mind reeling. Where were her parents? Who were those people who were after her? How could she move things with just her mind? And, where did Kai... the robot come from?

Answers evaded her, just like her childhood memories.

In less than a heartbeat, Eden sat up straight. Curling the quilt around her body, she tiptoed down the hall and into the living room. There was one thing she knew; she didn't want to be alone.

Kai was sound asleep on the futon, eyes twitching. Eden dragged her chair closer to him, watching his face as the black, wooden legs scraped against floorboards. When the chair was close enough for her liking, she curled her body into it, eyes still on Kai. Could it really have been the boy she'd dreamed of every night?

A tear warmed Eden's cheek as it fell. She quickly wiped it away. Something inside of her didn't want to believe it—that memory was painful, for both him and her. He was back in her life, with no answers of his own. The thought of living through that again scared the hell out of her. And as she stared at where the silver streak in his hair once was, she convinced herself it was all a lie. He wasn't really Kai. It was a trick that her parents created to try to get her memories back.

9

Eden

In the basement parking lot, Eden had stopped midway to her parent's car. She sighed with relief at the vacant spot meant for Zahra and Kobe's family car. Continuing on, she walked to section 7 and found her parents' car.

"Is it autopilot or manual?" Kai asked as he casually opened the passenger door.

Bewildered, Eden paused before hopping into the driver's side. "How do you—?"

Kai laughed before she got the sentence out. "I remembered a few things last night."

Pressing the "on" button, Eden said, "This is autopilot."

She punched in the coordinates to the New York, New Jersey border and sat back to put her seat belt on.

As the car began rolling toward the garage exit, Kai looked out the window. "I'm pretty sure I know how to drive an old manual."

"Scissors, no. Driving, yes," Eden teased, shaking her head.

She pressed a button on the side of the door and the window slid down at the same time the car halted. Eden leaned out and entered the passcode on a keypad mounted to the wall. The boom gate promptly flew up.

As they merged onto the street, Kai leaned forward, seeing the city in the daylight for the first time. His eyes crinkled at their edges, familiarity crossing his face. He sat back and turned to Eden. "Someone taught me how to drive, here in this city. It was recent, I think. He was older, had a beard." Kai squeezed his chin and furrowed his brow. "I can't remember his name."

Eden smiled in sympathy. "It sucks, doesn't it? Like you know something is there, you can feel it and sense it, but you can't see it."

Kai sighed and turned back to the window, letting his forehead rest on the glass.

"What else did you remember last night?" she asked, actually interested.

Kai rolled his head back around, showing a saddened expression. "I remembered you. Crying."

Eden let her eyes bounce between his. She swallowed. His aqua irises looked brighter than the day before. Deeper, more knowing.

"There was this wall between us," Kai continued. "Invisible, yet strong."

"Glass," Eden interrupted. "It was glass."

"Yes. I remember you. Behind glass."

They stared at each other for a moment, caught in a vision neither could escape from. Eden was terrified at the lengths her father went to ensure this version of Kai was identical to *her* Kai. But she'd never told her father how she felt in that memory—pain. And, right then, in this boy's eyes, pain was all she could see.

Blinking rapidly, she turned her attention to the

road—even though she didn't have to with the car on autopilot. Changing the subject, she asked, "You have the passports?"

"Yep." Kai waved both booklets loosely in his hands.

"Okay, when we get to the checkpoint, act normal."

An easy laugh tumbled from his voice box. "What's normal?"

Although ended, the sound of his laugh, a boisterous cackle, reverberated through her veins like a hurricane. Neurons sparked in her brain, sending her down a path she'd searched for but could never find. There it was right in front of her.

His laugh had triggered a memory…

She was in a kayak on Lake Louise. Eden peered over her shoulder at a smiley face sitting behind her. There he was, young and bright-eyed. Her heart soared at the sight of him. They were more than just friends. He was her best friend. Her soul mate.

His mouth curled up on one side, his favorite kind of smile to do. And he clutched either side of the kayak, knuckles turning white as he rocked from side to side.

"Stop!" Eden cried, trying not to laugh. She was holding on for dear life, as though falling in the water was a fate worse than death. "I don't want to swim today."

Twelve-year-old Kai grinned and gave the boat one more big tilt.

Losing her balance, Eden was flung to the side. She managed to catch herself, clambering to the higher side of the kayak to avoid falling in. Kai stopped laughing and leaned forward, holding his hand out.

Through slit eyes, she glared at him in fake fury. He was all things annoying and silly and downright cheeky but she'd never been mad at him. Even though he'd just been a complete dunderhead, she didn't hesitate to take his hand.

"Edie?" he asked, head tilted.

His voice sounded muffled, audible yet far away. Eden frowned in confusion. She pulled on his hand to bring him closer.

"Edie?" he said again. This time when his twelve-year-old mouth moved, a deeper, matured voice came out.

Eden shook her head as the memory made way for reality. The lake turned to city, and the kayak turned into a car. She stared at the eighteen-year-old version of Kai beside her.

His gaze went beyond her and he nodded a few times quickly. As he turned his attention back to Eden, he glanced briefly down in the space between them. "Edie?"

She followed his eyes and found her fingers folded through his. She whipped her hand free. "Uh, sorry."

His mouth curled up on one side. "What's that look for?"

"I..." she stuttered, still staring. "I remembered something."

His smile waned, still there yet more serious. Nodding once, he stated, "Good. But first things first, there's someone at our window."

Eden spun in her seat. It was then she realized the car had stopped moving. A border guard stood outside the car, tapping his knuckles against the glass.

As she let the window down, Kai whispered, "Just act normal."

"Passports," the guard demanded.

"Uh, yeah, sure." Eden cleared her throat, thrusting her arm in Kai's direction. He still had a tiny smirk on his face as he gently placed the passports into her palm.

The guard looked over the documents and photos, taking a moment to compare them with the delinquents in the car. "You're on your provisionals?"

he asked, flipping through Eden's passport. She'd only gotten a few stamps. Connecticut and Vermont mostly for holidays. It was her first time to New Jersey.

"Uhhh..." she hesitated.

Kai leaned forward and reached his hand out. "Yeah, I'm on my full license though, so that's okay, isn't it? I can drive a manual too, if that helps?"

"That's irrelevant," she hissed in a whisper, pushing him back. She turned back to the guard. "Yes, I'm provisional, but like he said, he's on his full license. Manual and all."

"That's exactly what I just said," Kai teased.

Eden waved her hand for him to be quiet as the guard snapped their passports shut. He tapped them on the edge of the car door. "One moment, we need to check your registration through the system."

"It's my dad's car!" Eden called after him. Watching the guard walk to his station, panic washed over her. "Shit. They're gonna think I stole the car. Or that you kidnapped me. They're gonna notice you're a robot for sure—"

"Hey!"

"Where will they take us? To jail? Oh God, what if I blast them without control?" Eden raised her hands in front of her, looking at them as though they were time bombs about to explode. "They'll think I'm a demon."

Kai reached for her hands and lowered them. With a calming tone, he said, "Chill, Edie. We've got this. Act normal, remember?"

Eden checked out the guard's reflection in her mirror as he marched from his station back to the car. He patted the passports against his palm like an old teacher would a paddle.

Wincing, Eden moaned, "I'm too young to go to jail."

Eden heard Kai chuckle beside her as the guard bent down. He rested the passports against the open window ledge. "I thought you said it was your dad's car."

Eden nodded vehemently. "Yes, it is. I swear."

"Well, it must be nice for a rich kid like you. Daddy put the car in your name. You're free to go. Enjoy New Jersey."

A red light in front of them turned green and the car began rolling again. Eden rushed to type in the next address from her parent's secret contact book. Settling back into the seat, she watched the border checkpoint become a dot in the distance.

Eden

The car came to a halt outside a two-story, red-bricked house. The outside was charming. A row of roses hugged the house's edge, a small oak shaded the front yard, and a sweet cobblestone path weaved from the sidewalk to the front entrance.

Eden jumped out of the car, marveling at the homestead. Waiting at the end of the path, she looked up to the second floor. A curtain flicked open and a young teen with long platinum blond hair peered down at them. Eden smiled at the girl; but she wasn't looking in Eden's direction, she was staring at Kai. Eden glanced over her shoulder as he caught up. She couldn't blame the girl; he was rather good-looking.

Together, they walked to the front door, wasting no time to knock.

The door creaked open and a lady with an auburn pixie crop and plump cheeks peered through the crack. When she noticed them standing there, her eyes lit with recognition. She threw the door wide open. "I didn't expect to see the two of you."

"You know me?" Kai asked, pointing to himself.

Ignoring him, the lady ran her eyes over Eden. "Fascinating"

Eden threw a thumb in Kai's direction. "Uh, he's the experiment, not me."

"Neither of you are experiments." The woman smiled. It wasn't a warm or inviting smile, but it was a smile all the same. She stepped to the side. "I'm Nancy. Come with me."

The foyer was pristine. Gold architraves swept along the ceiling. Marbled tiles led to a staircase that curved up onto a mezzanine. Eden wandered into the middle of the foyer, taking in all the art deco paintings that lined the walls.

Nancy closed the door behind them. "Do you want to see your parents? I know the safe house they are hiding in."

"Yes!" Eden blurted, spinning around. "They're safe? You've spoken with them?"

"Yes, I've spoken with them." Chuckling to herself, Nancy wandered into the lounge room. She glanced over her shoulder as if to make sure they were following. "Listen, it's probably a good idea to stay here, with me. I'll get in contact with your parents and organize a reunion." She curved her hands over the back of a floral sofa. "Sit down."

Eden threw herself onto the seat, her thighs bouncing a few times on top of the plush cushion. Kai remained standing, wrinkles forming between his brow. He glanced at Eden, then to the immaculate fireplace, then to the foyer.

"Sit, boy, sit." Nancy waved her hand at the sofa and spun on her heels. "I'll fetch us some tea."

She waddled out of the room, leaving Kai and Eden alone.

Eden bounced on the sofa again. "This is amazing."

Still scanning the house, Kai pulled at the bottom of his shirt. "I don't know if it's a good idea to stay here."

"Of course, it is. She's obviously a friend. It's all going to be fine from here on in."

Kai flipped his head to her, his eyes a deeper shade. He crossed his arms against his chest, hands balling into fists. "I don't want to be here, Eden."

It was strange to Eden, seeing him so afraid. Was it a memory or instinct that made his nerves rise?

Nancy returned to the room; her hands dug deep into her pant pockets. As Eden wondered where the tea was, Nancy's voice boomed, "Sit down, Malakai." She stopped herself halfway across the room and jerked her head to the side. After clearing her throat, she said with a softer voice, "Make yourself at home."

Something about the way Nancy moved reminded her of those demons. Is that what Kai thought, too. She turned to him.

He looked back with a pleading look in his eyes. "Edie, I don't like it."

"Okay," Eden agreed without hesitation. She stood up. "Thank you for your hospitality, Nancy. But we won't stay. Maybe you can tell my parents to meet us somewhere else?"

"Don't be ridiculous." Nancy frowned, straightening her head. From where she stood, Eden could have sworn she saw a small forked line zigzag up her neck.

Nancy pulled her hands out of her pockets, holding onto two bronze bracelets. They were identical to the ones the demons had the night before. She rushed toward Kai.

Eden's heart skipped a beat as Nancy closed the gap within a second. Hand out, Nancy aimed the bracelet for Kai's wrist. Quick like lightning, he clutched her shoulders and pushed, sending her flying across the room. Right before Nancy crashed into a hardwood piano, Eden threw her arm out.

She held Nancy, hovering above the ivory keys. Even if she looked a little like the demons, she looked like a human, too, and that was enough for Eden to want to protect her. She lowered the woman to the floor, saying to Kai, "Let's go."

Kai ran to the door and Eden scurried to keep up. When he reached the door, he turned back to Eden. Eyes widening, he cried, "No! Edie look out she's—"

A sharp pain crossed the back of Eden's skull. She blinked slowly, watching Kai run to her in blurry motion. Then, everything went black.

Kai

A dull pain, like muscles tightening, spread across Kai's upper back. He stretched his arms across his body, as far as he could in a small car, to release some pressure. He was careful not to knock Eden, who was sleeping peacefully beside him. It was a shame she looked like that because of the vicious actions of a monster.

Kai leaned over and pressed his fingers at the base of her skull. He pulled his hand away to check for blood, happy to see that she was healing just fine. Sighing, he rolled down the car window and turned his face to the cool breeze.

He knew Nancy Withers was evil, he could sense it from the moment he stepped foot into her house. Her face seemed familiar and the sight of her was accompanied by a sinking stomach. He didn't know much, but he knew those weren't good signs.

He almost wished he finished her off back there, but getting Eden away was his priority. Once Nancy knocked Eden over the head with a vase and he watched her tumble to the ground, his only desire was to get the hell out of there. So, he pushed Nancy as hard as he could and when he was happy with the distance between them, he scooped Eden in his arms and ran.

Now, he was sitting in the car with her somewhere between New Jersey and God knows where. The car stopped about an hour earlier, out of gas or juice or whatever it was that fueled an autopilot vehicle.

He knew her better than he had earlier, too. The wait bringing little snippets of his life to the surface. Every moment he recalled, her face was always there, smiling, teasing, shining.

A soft groan wisped into the air beside him. Kai swung around, heart in his throat. Eden opened her eyes one at a time.

"What happened?" she said groggily, rubbing her head.

"Oh, just a demon, a vase, and an excellent getaway, that's all," Kai chirped, hoping not to worry her.

Eden blinked a few times as if trying to grasp her surroundings. She rolled her head to Kai and mumbled, "Did you get the girl?"

"Nancy?" Kai licked his lips, ready to tell her the whole story of how he saved her ass. "Oh yeah, I showed that bitc—"

"No." Eden frowned, resting her head back onto the seat. "The other one."

What was she talking about? Kai placed the back of his hand against her forehead. "Maybe she knocked you harder than I thought."

Watching her eyes roll, Kai panicked. He fumbled with the door handle, wondering how on earth he'd get her to a hospital before nightfall. He muttered to himself, "You're an idiot, Malakai. She's delirious."

"Shut up, you're delirious." Eden scoffed.

Kai's fingers released from the door handle, his

heart resting. That sounded like the real Eden. Maybe she was okay after all.

Seeming a little brighter, Eden glanced around. "Where are we? Why are we not moving?" A slight teasing smile flashed as she said, "Did you realize you don't know how to drive?"

"The car just stopped."

Eden sat up straight. "Dammit, I didn't think to charge it. How long have we been stopped for?"

"An hour or two. I don't know." Kai shrugged. He reached down between the dashboard and pulled out a brown bag. "I got you a burger."

Eden's brows fell to her eyes, she whipped her head in every direction. "When?"

The confusion on her face amused him. It was followed immediately with guilt for finding her discomfort funny. She did look cute though, with her doe eyes and scrunched up nose.

"Kai? Hello? When did you get the burger?"

He shook his head, realizing he'd been staring. Throwing a hand over his shoulder, he said, "Uh, I saw a drive-thru, just out of Stanton. I thought you might be hungry when you woke up."

Kai stuffed his hand into the bag and pulled a burger out. It was cold but he hoped she was hungry enough not to care. He watched her unwrap it, lift the bun to her nose, and promptly bite down. Satisfied that she was happy, he took his own burger out.

Eden's eyes lifted, still holding the burger to her mouth. "Why didn't you eat before?"

"I wanted to wait for you. It felt rude."

Her nose did that adorable scrunch thing, again. She tore her eyes off him, declaring, "You're too nice."

Kai let out a guffaw. "That's the first time you've ever called me nice. It's normally knuckle-dragger or dimwit or meatball."

"How..." Eden looked at him sideways. "How would you know?"

The point between his blades ached. Rolling his shoulders, he said, "Memories."

"Yeah?" Eden's eyes landed on his back. "What kind?"

A soft smile lifted the edges of his mouth. "*Nice* ones."

Heat turned Eden's cheeks red. Without looking at him, she opened the car door and stepped outside. Kai watched her begin marching down the highway.

Kai couldn't help himself, he liked seeing her squirm. Nothing malicious, of course. Going by the things he remembered, it was just something they did —tease each other. Smirking, he jumped out of the car and ran to catch up with her.

"If we want to get to New York before curfew, we need to hurry," she said before taking a piece of lettuce between her teeth and sliding it out of the bun.

Still smiling, Kai bit into his burger. Even though it was cold, he slowed his pace to enjoy the first taste. With his mouth full, he said, "I forgot how good these were."

Eden shoved her hand over her mouth to stop the piece of lettuce from falling out. She swallowed quickly. "You've no idea, Robot. Wait for pizza and nougat and—"

"Caramel, your favorite."

Eden glanced at him.

He winked in return, and with a voice deeper than normal, he said, "I told you, I'm not a robot."

Cheeks flushing, she looked ahead. Her feet churned along the pavement as she scarfed the rest of her meal.

Kai knew then that it was more than the childhood banter it used to be. He could render her speechless by a mere few words or a small glance. He affected her. A weird feeling stirred inside his chest and he couldn't quite pinpoint what it meant.

The walk to the border was silent—Eden leading,

Kai a few steps behind. He gazed at the not too distant skyline of New York. The late afternoon sun shone through Eden's hair that bounced against her face as she walked, her dyed streak shining behind the light. She tucked her hair behind her ear and Kai smiled as it fell back over her cheek.

As the border came into view, Kai found himself watching the guards stop cars. It was strange. In all the clear moments he had remembered, curfew or state patrol or drones weren't in any of them.

There was a pattern. Each car was stopped for five minutes, passports and registrations were checked, then the travelers were sent on their merry way. So, it caught his eye when one car had been left sitting for at least ten minutes already. Quietly, and without fuss, several guards made their way to the car. The trunk was forced open and a young boy, around the age of twelve, was dragged out.

Kai's pace sped up.

The boy had light blond hair, almost white—it sat on his head in a Mohawk, reaching for the sky. A guard began to pull him toward the patrol house and his parents screamed. The boy thrashed in their hold and as his head shook, Kai caught sight of his eyes. Bright green. As a guard slapped cuffs around his wrists, the color faded.

They thought the boy was a demon, that was for sure. The guards were doing their duty by reprimanding him, but something deep inside of Kai was repulsed by the way they were treating him. He tightened his fists, a bubble in his stomach rising.

Eden's delicate fingers curved over his shoulder. "We can't do anything. Look at all those guards."

"He's just a kid," Kai argued.

She ran her hand down to his elbow, and he watched her movements. "Listen, all I know is that the guards have authority to take anyone they see fit and anyone who sympathizes is incarcerated. Do you really want to be locked up over a stranger?"

Kai looked back to the guards, now taking the boy's parents inside the patrol building. It wasn't right. The boy, the border, curfew. None of it felt right.

They slowed their pace as they approached the checkpoint. To the right, the Statue of Liberty stood tall, lifting her light to the world. Below her, drones were lined up charging for their night patrol.

As they waited in line, Eden bounced on her feet. "I'm not so sure we're going to make it all the way home by the time the sun sets."

People were sparse, rushing for their homes, even the cars driving through the checkpoint came in slow drawn out waves. Nevertheless, they strolled up to the guard and handed her their passports as if they were out for a late afternoon stroll.

"Where you headed?" the guard asked, looking between their faces and their passports.

"Home," Eden said at the same time Kai said, "visiting a friend."

Eden gave a nervous laugh. "My home. I'm the visited friend."

The guard handed their passports back. "It's close to curfew."

"That's okay, we'll make it," Eden enthused, putting on her cheeriest smile.

Kai bit his lip, knowing her true thoughts on that matter. He cleared his throat. "Yeah, she doesn't live too far."

The guard shrugged, nonchalant. "It's your funeral. The walking gate for the tunnel is to the left."

Kai

Night fell quickly. The half-moon hovered directly above them as they walked through Lower Manhattan, still a long way from home. Doors were locked and lights were flicked on. Indoors became full of life, while outside became breathless. Within moments, Kai and Eden remained the only living beings in the streets.

Not too far away, the sound of drones began scattering around them. It was only a matter of time before they were caught. Kai felt Eden's hand slip into his. It would have been a nice moment if her next movement wasn't to drag him up the front stairs of the closest building. She pushed him into the doorway, her body close beside him. Safely hidden by shadows, she lifted her watch. Their dots pulsated where they stood, Eden's a pale shade and Kai's a brighter blue. Around them, the white dots of the drones spread out across New York. Eden zoomed out and trailed the path over the Brooklyn Bridge to her home.

Kai was relieved not to see any red dots showing on the map at all. But there was something else. Two more dots. They were a darker shade of blue, almost navy like the night sky above them. The new dots were at City Hall Park, only a few blocks away. And they were moving fast in their direction.

"We have to use the Manhattan Bridge," Eden said, stepping out of the shadows. She checked her watch again and as a drone passed the next street over she began jogging down the stairs. Looking over her shoulder, she called out, "Now!"

It didn't take long for Kai to catch up to her. Not wanting to put his whole trust in the watch, he rushed past Eden and went ahead to check the following street. He stopped at the edge and peered around the corner. Eden closed in behind him, taking the reprieve to check her watch again.

Kai stood a head above her, looking down at her watch. The dark blue dots were coming in fast. Eden and Kai had moved across two blocks running as fast as they could, but these dots, they were moving at a monumental speed, already covering four blocks in the same amount of time. The dots now stood between them and their path to the Manhattan Bridge.

"What are they?" Eden rasped, staring down the darkened street.

Demons, Kai thought, but he didn't want to scare her. He tapped the projection and moved the map along to the Williamsburg Bridge. "There aren't many drones this way?"

Eden shook her head. "We're running toward them now, we might have to just head north. There might be hiding spots in Central Park where we can stay?"

Hands to his head, Kai turned in a circle. A curse word flew out of his mouth, natural and effortless. He winced and looked back at the watch. The dark blue dots had made more ground since they'd stopped. "Okay, fine. We gotta go now, though."

He clutched her wrist and dragged her up Broadway. Kai tore down the street, faster than Eden could run. A sudden urge took over him, he wanted to lift off the ground, feel the wind on his face, find a gap between the pavement and the sky.

Déjà vu hit and a memory soon followed. Times Square, with Eden by his side. But this time they weren't scrambling along the ground, they were... flying.

The night air was cool as it hit his face. A sense of freedom rippled through his being. Below him the streets were alive, car lights hitting bumpers, one in front of the other. People were staring, as one might expect if they saw a person with wings for the first time.

As he soared through Times Square, he extended his arm at full stretch. His fingers grazed the arm of another. Twisting his head, his eyes landed on Eden. Her twelve-year-old smile, lit her half-baby, half-grown face. He tapped his fingers against her skin playfully and surged forward. Looking back, he watched her wings spread wide. The wind whipped through her black and white feathers. Her wings were always a sight to behold—obsidian at the base that gradually turned to ivory at their tips.

He rolled his shoulders, feeling the weight of his wings, their power propelling him onward. Together, the two of them swooped above the growing crowd, their shadows casting odd shapes below. Cameras flashed, and they laughed. Finally, he could show his true colors, be who he was without any second thought. The humans deserved to know who they were, and they needed to know what was happening to their kind.

There was a sense of justice alongside the joy.

If they showed humans they existed, they could show humans the injustice that was happening to them.

Wings and hearts open, they kept soaring out of New York. Laughing and spinning all the way north.

They kept flying until they reached their hideout. A remote set of barns in Alberta, Canada.

Kai gasped back into the present moment. The heaviness of his stride along the street weighed down on his heart. He turned to find Eden a few yards behind him. As she ran, Eden held the watch up. The dark blue dots had changed trajectory, speeding around the corner where Eden and Kai had just stood.

"They're following us," she puffed. Her eyes were as wide as they could go, staring at the watch.

Kai looked beyond her to where they came from. He felt all the blood drain from his face.

Two wolves. Golden tips at the end of their fur shimmered in the moonlight. They moved swiftly yet silently, toward them. As the pair of animals noticed them, they slowed their run into a prowl. Low, as though ready for the final charge.

"Edie?" Kai whispered, his tone a caution.

As she turned to see what he saw, Kai wrapped his arms around her and dragged her into a darkened alley. He took her as far back as they could go, right beside the stage entrance of a run-down theater. A rumble in the back of Kai's throat echoed up through the small space, bouncing off the red-bricked walls.

"Wait here," he said, letting Eden go.

He crept to the entrance of the alley and rested his palm against the brick. Breathing long and low, he waited. The overhead light of a flashing neon sign cast pink shadows across his face. It was an old sign, from times gone by. Safer times when people were allowed outside after dark and drones didn't scan the streets for curfew breakers. He took one more breath, his shoulders rising and falling dramatically, and peered around the corner.

"What are they doing?" Eden called from the end of the alley.

Two wolves, majestic and terrifying, prowled down the pavement about half a block away. Spotting Kai, they turned to him. He pushed himself off the wall and sprinted for Eden.

At the end of the alley, Kai stood in front of her like a bodyguard. With a wide stance, his muscles contracted, ready for war. "We can't outrun them."

"Why are they after us?" Eden asked, moving in behind him.

Kai's voice quaked, he glanced over his shoulder at her frightened face. "I remembered something."

"What?"

"Edie," he said, turning around slowly. "We're the reason for the curfew."

Instinct kicked in and Kai threw his body around Eden, placing both hands against the wall on either side of her head. Pain seared across his back. He lifted his face to the sky and moaned.

Behind him, two wings unfurled. Out of the corner of his eyes, he saw shimmering blue feathers, opalescent like a peacock. His wings spread so far the feathers spanned half of the alley.

Eden squeaked, "We can't be demons."

"We're not." Kai shook his head. "We're Angels."

13

Eden

Angels.

Eden stared at the wings attached to Kai's back.

Wings.

A flash of neon blue lit the rims of his irises.

Angels.

When she said they were demons, she didn't really mean it. But this... this sight of...

Wings...

It was something she had never even dreamed of.

Kai stood over her, wincing. He looked as scared as she felt. A soft patter of paws loomed on the street. Eden lifted the watch to see the wolves' dots just around the corner in front of the theater.

Noticing their proximity, Kai pushed himself off the wall and stood tall. Rolling his shoulders with balled fists, his wings folded in until there was no trace of them at all.

"What do we do?" she whispered.

Hands clasped at the nape of his neck; Kai moved

his head in every direction. Front, back, left, right... up. His eyes remained on the sky as he said, "Climb."

"Climb?" Eden guffawed. The wall was made of bricks, how on earth could they manage to traverse it?

"You don't know how to climb?" Kai gave a half-frown, half-smile.

"Not up a freaking wall. It's ninety degrees."

Kai shrugged and patted his back. "I'll have to carry you then."

The request made Eden's heart leap. She inhaled too quickly, spluttering out the excess air. Why did he do that to her? Always making her a crumbling mess. Eden blamed it on the lack of sleep and proper nutrition. Frowning, she shook her head. "Not gonna do that."

Shadows of long, pointed ears stretched out in front of the alleyway. Kai whipped his head around and hissed, "What other choice do you have?"

Eden leaped onto his back. He stood still as her chest pressed against him. His arms held her legs for a moment and he twisted his face. As his eyes found hers, his breath changed. Instead of being sure and sturdy, it was broken and shaky. Eden swallowed, his gaze dropped to her lips and back up again.

For a moment, she was jealous of his memories. The way he looked at her indicated he knew something secret about her. Something that made him protective of her.

The wolves slid into the alleyway and Kai straightened himself. As he reached for the edge of the brick wall, the thump of running paws, echoed down the alley. Right when the wolves pounced, Kai hauled them up the wall. Below them, the wolves jumped, fangs snapping at their heels. Kai was too fast, though. Effortlessly, he scaled the side of the building. One meter, two meters, three.

Stalking on the ground, the wolves below them became lost in the shadows. Eden relaxed and pulled herself back a little, studying the space where his wings had just been. "I have a question."

"Mmm?" Kai murmured.

"You have wings and we're climbing?"

He tilted his head still climbing. "Would you rather clutch onto my back or front?"

Again, her heart soared. She hated how he affected her; it made her feel vulnerable, and everybody knew she didn't do vulnerability. Being vulnerable was the worst. It was like sadness and blood-shot eyes and guilt. Eden cleared her throat, then muttered, "Back will do."

They reached the top of the six-story playhouse. Eden climbed off Kai's back and they both peered over the edge of the building. The two wolves emerged out of the shadow, except not wolves anymore, people. Two of them, side by side scaling the wall just like Kai did.

Kai stepped away from the edge. "We have no choice. I'm sorry, Edie."

"What are you sorry for—"

Kai tucked one arm under Eden's knees and slid another under her armpit. He lifted her up, and holding her against his chest, he unfurled his wings. Eden clutched his neck as his feet left the roof. She gasped and squeezed her eyes shut, tucking her head into his collarbone.

His laugh rumbled against her ear. "You could fly, too, y'know?"

Could she? Could she really?

Taking a quick inhale full of bravery, Eden opened her eyes. She looked behind them, seeing the wolf-people reach the roof. They were already a block away, and lower than she thought they would be, sweeping around the top floors of buildings. Drones buzzed below them, oblivious to anything above. Letting one hand fall from his neck, her arm dropped by her side. The air was cold, but something about the way it swept through her fingers, made her feel alive. It felt like freedom. Like the way it was meant to be.

As Kai surged up, they swooped through a wispy cloud. Eden threw her hand back, clutching onto him.

"It's okay," Kai whispered. "I won't let you go. Just like you would never let me go."

Eden turned her head to find him smiling at her. The way he looked at her spread warmth from her heart through all her limbs. A sense of familiarity rose. She'd had a small glimpse of this boy, little memories flitting through her mind. She knew his name. She knew they were close. She knew she cared about him. Too much sometimes, enough to scare her... enough to pretend he wasn't real. But how? Why? She knew he had the answer to that.

Kai landed on the top of Eden's apartment building and lowered her gently until her feet were safely on the roof. She glanced quickly at the shattered conservatory and the dead bodies still inside. Drones hovered nearby, their searchlights circling dangerously close.

"Forget about them, Edie. Come on." Kai placed his hand on her lower back and guided her into the internal stairwell door.

They moved down two flights in silence.

Back aching, Eden stopped at the seventh-floor door. The projected blueprint of her apartment showed nothing out of the ordinary. Aside from the white dots of the drones scanning the streets, the only lights that glowed on the watch belonged to her and Kai. She noticed that Kai's light was now significantly darker and brighter than hers.

At any other moment, it would have been a question. But she was too tired, her brain too full of questions that one more felt like it could shatter her from the inside out. So, she didn't say anything, instead, she opened the door and headed for her ransacked home.

Inside, she marched down the hallway straight for her bedroom. The room had been turned upside down and the shock of it made her knees weak. Eden knew she shouldn't have been surprised but still, she was. Someone had been in her house, again. Ignoring the pang in her chest, she grabbed the edge of her upturned mattress and pulled. It was heavier than expected.

She looked over her shoulder to find Kai taking in her bedroom. It was darker than most rooms, walls painted maroon. There was a splattering of glow in the dark stickers on the ceiling and posters of the night sky in various spots across the room. Eden loved her room. But it didn't matter anymore.

"A little help here, please?" she huffed.

"Oh." Kai tore his eyes from a blue-green galaxy poster and clasped the other edge of the mattress. "Where are we taking it?"

Eden stuffed two pillows under her arm. "To the lab."

They twisted the mattress through the doorframe and carried it down the hallway to the office. Kai could have carried the whole thing by himself, Eden barely had a grip on it as he moved up the stairs. He dropped the mattress on the cold lab floor and Eden threw the pillows on top of it.

"It's a good idea, Edie," Kai said straightening the pillows. "This place is like a fortress."

She nodded once, pleased with herself. "I'll be right back."

A quick run to the kitchen, her parents' room, and her own room again, and Eden had managed to gather two peanut butter and jelly sandwiches, a pair of her father's pajama bottoms for Kai, and her own pajamas for herself. Arms full, she climbed the stairs. Halfway up she saw Kai had pushed the mattress into the corner and was standing back with his arms crossed.

As she entered the lab, he whipped his head

around. "Does it look okay there?"

Eden emptied the contents of her hands onto her quilt. "It's a mattress in a lab. It doesn't matter about looks."

"I just want you to be comfortable."

Sweet rush. From her chest to her cheeks. She swiveled around and hit the button at the top of the stairs. The bookshelf at the bottom slid across, clicking shut.

Brushing past Kai, Eden fell onto the mattress. She grabbed a sandwich and stuffed it into her mouth. As Kai sat across from her, she avoided eye contact and said, "Thank you."

"What for?" he asked, taking the other sandwich.

Eyes on the half-eaten bread in her hands, Eden smiled. "For keeping me safe today—with the wolves and the drones and Nancy."

Kai swallowed. "It's what we do."

Brows falling, Eden dropped her hands to her lap. For the first time in a while, she met his gaze. "What did you mean before? When you said we were the ones who caused curfew?"

"Doesn't matter." Kai shrugged and shoved the last of his dinner into his mouth.

"It kind of does."

Eyeing the sandwich still in her grasp, he said, "You'll remember it soon."

"I'm so tired of trying to remember things." Eden huffed, passing him the rest of her sandwich. She threw her body backward and lifted her watch to check on the activity. Two blue dots blinked on the screen, one darker than the other. Raking her hands through her hair, she stared at the ceiling.

After polishing off Eden's sandwich, Kai moved down and rested his elbow on the mattress. "What *do* you remember?"

Eden gave a small laugh and propped herself up on her elbows. "I guess it is that time of night."

"Huh?"

"Oh, it doesn't matter." She rolled onto her stomach and picked at the edge of the pillowcase. "Just something my parents did every night at six o'clock. An interrogation of sorts. It was painful."

Kai let his elbow collapse under him and he lay on his side, facing Eden. Deep creases wrinkled across his forehead in sympathy. "Painful?"

He was inches away. Those aqua eyes staring at her with intensity, with care, with concern. Looking at him made her feel helpless. Like a constant pane of glass was between them. Even memories couldn't shatter.

"Being torn from..." Eden stopped herself from saying "you." Still too frightened to admit who he was. Someone that meant something to her and was taken away for six years. Looking at him felt like both everything and nothing. His eyes brought a hollowness. Like a void too big to fill. If she let him in, just a small amount... if she let him fill the lost part of her, what then would it feel like to lose him all over again?

He reached for her, hand clasping her shoulder. "What are you remembering?"

"Losing my best friend."

Kai nodded. "I'm here now."

Eden sat up, feeling the tears reach her eyes. She shook her head and turned her back to him. "I never said you were my best friend, Robot."

He didn't reply. Instead, Eden felt his hand drop from her shoulder, a sigh filling the small space they occupied.

Eden wiped her face, stood up, and picked up her pajamas. With her chin to her shoulder, she said, "Don't look."

After she changed her clothes, she turned to find Kai facing the other way. He had put on her father's pajama pants and was sitting bare-chested with his knees up, elbows resting over them. Eden imagined herself scooting in behind him, sliding her arms along his biceps. Her heart flipped, and she scolded herself for having such ridiculous thoughts.

"I'm done," she said, lying back down.

Kai shifted, a quick glance to make sure it was safe to turn around. His eyes met hers, a burst of aqua brightening the stark room. Quieting her annoying, soaring heart, Eden rolled the other way and tucked her hands under her cheek.

It was too late. She already cared. Losing him now would feel like a limb being torn from her body. It was utterly insane to feel that way about a stranger. The truth was, she knew he wasn't a stranger at all.

Almost resigning to her vulnerability, Eden sighed and looked around the clinical room. It was nothing at all like the homey part of their apartment below. How could she have lived so freely before? She was too wrapped up in finding that speck of light in her own shadows, that she couldn't see the secret room right under her nose. Or rather, above her head.

Something colorful caught her eye. Underneath the steel bed, resting against a back leg was a vial full of blue liquid. Eden forced herself from the mattress and crawled to retrieve it. Returning to the mattress, she held the vial up to the fluorescent light.

"I've seen that before," Kai said, holding his hand out.

Eden placed the vial onto his palm. "What is it?"

"Your father injected me with this stuff. Right before he let me come downstairs to you."

"He injected that stuff into you?" Eden squinted and move closer, trying to get a better look. "What is it?"

Kai held the vial between two fingers and twisted his hand over and back as though he was shaking a snow globe. "He said it would help my grace return."

"Grace?" Eden sat back. "'Cause you're an Angel?"

Pointing between them, Kai said, "We're Angels."

Eden shook her head. It was weird to have someone tell you what you were, despite not knowing it fully for yourself. She kneaded her fingertips in the space between her shoulder blades. Maybe that's why her parents never told her what she was, because they knew she couldn't truly understand it until her whole memory returned.

"Hey," Kai said, tapping her watch. "Do you think that's what the blue dots mean? Red is demon, blue must be Angel."

"Uh, those things that hunted us on the streets were blue. I doubt werewolves are Angels, Kai!" Eden teased.

An easy laugh tumbled from his lips.

"What?" Eden thwacked his thigh playfully. "How is that funny?"

"You called me Kai."

Eden

Damn her father for bringing that *boy* into her life, making her feel things.

Unable to sleep Eden lay on her back, thinking about how that boy said they were Angels. And while she had to admit that the notion was a little exciting, she couldn't see how it was possible. She stared at her hands. Hands that could move things just by a thought. Eden sat up, a strange idea coming to her. Keeping her hands to her side, she looked at the broken picture frame lying face down next to the computer.

Move, she thought, bunching her quilt into her fists.

The frame wobbled on the spot and lifted off the table. Eden imagined it flipping and placing itself on the table upright. No effort. Behind a crack, a photo of twelve-year-old Eden and her parents sat perfectly, displaying itself to the room. She quickly flipped the photo face down.

It wasn't her hands after all. It was just, *her.* Eden, the Angel.

A flash of pain ran up her spine, settling in between her shoulder blades. As she lifted her hand to give herself a massage, she noticed her watch flashing. The time said eight in the evening. It felt so much later. She tapped the button and brought up the blueprint where two blue dots occupied the lab. Two more dots, dark blue like the wolves', were pacing inside her father's study.

"Robot!" she screamed as the sound of steel bending echoed up the stairs.

In an urge to defend, she rushed to the top of the stairs. Kai must have felt the same because within a split second he was right beside her. At one end of the stairwell, two young Angels dampened by memory loss stared with fear at the other end. And at the bottom of the stairwell, a wolf began shifting into human form.

The human stepped out of the shadows up to the first step. Not a demon. A friend.

"Thank God, you're safe," Zahra said, a golden glimmer in her eyes.

A wolf leaped from the study into the space beside her. With a shake of its head, it began shifting from an animal to a person. Next to Zahra, stood her twin brother, Kobe.

"Hi, Eeeds," Kobe said, sheepishly running his hand around the back of his head.

Eden eyed them, confusion falling. Zahra and Kobe, her friends, they were the wolves from earlier. The thought tore through her stomach. She stepped backward, letting Kai stand in front of her.

"Oh no, don't do that. We're here to take you home." Zahra held her hands in surrender, moving slowly up the stairs. "It's me Eden, your best friend."

"I am home," Eden replied, reaching for Kai. She clutched onto his wrist and tugged him back away from Zahra.

"No, to your real home. The one you've been missing." Zahra entered the lab. There was a softness in her tone. "Remember when you had that dream about this magical place, far away? You told me it gave you a feeling of safety and comfort."

Eden swallowed. Of course, Zahra would use her own vulnerability against her.

Zahra continued, "Cornfields? Mountains hugging a valley? Rolling hills? Warm midday sun? It's not a dream, Eden, it's real."

Kobe entered the lab next, strategically placing himself behind Zahra. Kai jolted. He flung his palm to his chest as if asking himself who to trust.

"Check the watch," Zahra urged. "We're on your side."

Eden brought the screen up on her watch. Four blue dots flickered brightly, some different shades but blue all the same. Realization settled. Kai was right, blue dot meant Angel.

Zahra nodded, as though knowing what Eden was thinking. She took a step toward them. Eden rushed forward.

A tight grip on her wrist stopped her mid-run. Kai pulled her back. He ran his eyes over the twins, then lowered them to Eden. "You trust them?"

"Yes." Eden released herself from his grasp and tapped his chest. "You can, too." She spun on her heels and leapt for Zahra, who greeted her with an exuberant hug.

Kobe ruffled his fingers through her locks. "Nice 'do, girl."

"Listen," Zahra said, pulling out of Eden's embrace. "We can't stay here. The drones are all over you. They spotted you in the streets, the authority will be here at first light. We need to be long gone by then."

Eden glanced back at a bare-chested Kai, wearing nothing but her father's pajama pants. She laughed at the Déjà vu. "Can we get dressed first?"

Eden was standing at the entrance of her apartment with Kobe and Zahra. She'd rushed to get dressed, putting on her ripped jeans and favorite tee—white with a black feather in the center. She gripped the backpack straps containing a few of her belongings around her shoulders and bounced on her heels as they waited for Kai.

As he stepped out to join them, Kobe looked Kai up and down. "Nice clothes, dude."

"Thanks." Kai beamed, trying to cover a bullet hole with his hand. "We stole them while on the run."

Eden chuckled to herself, knowing that she'd grabbed the shirt from the twins' clothesline. She shared an amused glance with Kobe as he said, "No kidding."

They headed down the corridor, bypassing the curfew-timed elevators. Their sprightly steps echoed down the stairwell as they descended.

"Sorry that we scared you," Zahra said.

Eden gave a teasing smile. "To be fair, you were wolves."

"We move faster as animals." Kobe mimicked her smile and grabbed the rail at the landing. He leaped over, touching down with a thud halfway along the next flight.

"Can all Angels do that?" Eden asked, peering over the edge to make sure Kobe was all right.

"Shift?" Zahra asked and before waiting for a response she said, "We call ourselves Nephilim actually, half Angel, half human. And no, only a few. Haven't you got your full memory back yet? I was hoping after your grace and abilities returned it would follow."

"Has it been that long since you went through the same thing, sister?" Kobe waited at the bottom of the second-floor stairs. "It takes a day or two until everything comes back."

Zahra shrugged and wrapped her arm around Eden, squeezing her in close. "Oh, well. She's on her way and that's all that matters." Loosening her grip a little, she explained, "Different Nephilim have different abilities depending on which Archangel they were born from."

Eden peered over her shoulder at Kai who was following close behind. "Because that clears things up."

A soft smile lit his face. She'd seen it a few times before, whenever he remembered something new, or old rather. She slid out from under Zahra's arm and waited for Kai to catch her step. She whispered, "Do you know what she's talking about?"

"Yes. Sort of." He winced. "I'm not sure. It just makes sense, like a piece of the puzzle has been put in place. Not quite a full picture, but something."

Eden dug her teeth into her lip and nodded. She understood. Just having him with her felt like half the puzzle was completed already.

As they bounded down the final flight of stairs, Eden gaped at Zahra's bobbing blond curls. For six years they'd been friends. They'd seen each other every day. They'd grown up together. Spent their teenage years together.

"And you've always been this way?" Eden asked the back of Zahra's head as she gleefully led them through the quiet apartment foyer.

"Always," Zahra replied, glancing over her shoulder with a twinkle in her eye. "Just like you have. Except, I've just known a little longer than you."

Kobe ran ahead a few meters and tapped on the entrance doors. They swung open, and a boy stepped in. Young, at least seventeen, and with the whitest, purest hair slicked back on his head. In contrition, he had dark lashes and kohl liner under his eyes. He was pretty but looked rough. There was a fresh cut on his lip, a glob of red threatened to coat his chin.

As the three of them caught up with Kobe, he swung his arm around the other boy's neck. "You remember Deacon?"

Eden and Kai stared at him blankly.

"No?" Kobe asked, then shrugged. "I guess you will soon. Well..." He eyed Kai's hair. "Maybe not you."

"Heh." Deacon scoffed, squinting at Kai. "Savior complex got warrior boy vaporized... again."

There was something about the way Deacon stood —chest out, one shoulder down, resting scowl face. There was something about Kobe, too, how relaxed he was next to Deacon. And Zahra, how she had a comfortable smile while her eyes flicked between them all. It was the five of them together... it mattered. Of course, she didn't know how or why, but it did. And she was happy with that.

"Now, now." Kobe flung a backhand onto Deacon's chest. "It's not his fault."

Deacon rolled his eyes and threw a thumb over his shoulder. He sighed first, and with a bored tone, said, "The hideout is this way. Stay close to me if you want to live."

He stepped out of the building onto the sidewalk, rolled his neck and unfurled two rose gold wings—the tips of his feathers shimmered as though metallic. Flapping his wings once, Deacon lifted off the ground. As the other four stepped outside, Deacon hovered above them and moved into the open street.

Shoulder to shoulder with Kai, Eden leaned back to eye the place where his wings had grown from. He looked at her sheepishly and gave a small smile. It almost seemed like an apology.

Zahra smiled as she watched Eden's expression. She linked her arm around Eden's elbow and began walking underneath Deacon. "We've so much to catch up on."

As they stepped out of the shadows and into the light, Eden froze. "Wait!" she cried, checking her watch. The white dot of a drone sped down the street right around the corner. Kai's breath warmed Eden's neck as he stared at the projection. Within a second, he'd grabbed her hand. The jolt of his hold made her spin from Zahra's keep.

"Oh, you two," Zahra said, trying not to laugh. She pointed up at Deacon. "He's a Shield Angel. Born of Chamuel, he protects us from anything that wishes to harm..." Her smile waned as she looked between their bewildered faces. "His power acts like invisibility, for himself and others. They can't see us."

"Come on," Deacon moaned with a scowl, his wings keeping him on the spot with harsh flicks. "They're waiting for us."

Eden followed the same drone that was on her watch spear down the sidewalk. She stepped out below it and Kai gasped behind her. The drone's light ran over her, Zahra, and Kobe, and without a peep, it continued down its path. Eden held her hand back for Kai and slowly, he placed his hand in hers.

They walked quickly through the abandoned streets of New York and Eden collected the pieces she had gathered along the way. Zahra and Kobe were Nephilim, shape-shifting Nephilim. And they always had been. They knew she was one, did her parents know, too? Of course, they did.

Following Deacon around a corner, Eden broke the silence. "Zahra? Do you know where my parents are?"

Zahra linked her arm back through Eden's. "No, sorry. After the Hunters came into the building, we hightailed it to here."

"Where?" Eden blinked, realizing she had no idea where they were. She glanced at Zahra's pointed finger and looked beyond it.

The Empire State Building.

Kai

"Excuse me for one second," Zahra said, walking to the entrance.

Kai could see her reflection in the door. Fangs grew where her teeth should be, three times their normal size, and she crunched them deep into her palm. A drop of blood ran across the lines in her hand and she placed it against the wall. Within seconds the door clicked open.

Wiping her mouth, Zahra turned and smiled. "Our blood is the key to the city. Or at least, this building."

Deacon pushed himself inside, marching down the marble floors, straight for the stairwell. Everyone followed Zahra, but Kai lagged behind, mesmerized by the gilded lobby. He walked with his eyes up, staring at the gold patterns that ran the length of the ceiling. He kept up with the others by the sound of their steps. When the noise stopped, he looked down to find Kobe holding open a door.

"We're headed this way, memory boy," Kobe said, holding a door open. As Kai, walked through Kobe slapped him on the shoulder. "You've been here countless times."

Eden was waiting for him at the top of the stairs. She held her hand out for him and he took it without question. As they moved down, Eden said, "Zahra? What you said before, about Hunters breaking into our apartment. Are they demons?"

Zahra stopped at the stairwell's turning point. She sighed and shared a glance with Kobe. "Worse. They're humans."

Recalling their obsidian eyes and dark blood, Kai didn't think they looked like humans. He asked, "Why are they hunting us? Because they think we're demons?"

"Oh no." Kobe laughed as he passed the three of them. As he sped on, he called over his shoulder, "They definitely know we're Nephilim."

"They want our grace," Kai stated, answering his own question. The words came at the same time the memory hit. A synchronized clashing of worlds.

"Bingo," Kobe crowed with his hand in the air, already down the next flight.

Eden's nose scrunched.

Zahra moved up a step to meet Eden and squeezed her shoulder. "I know you want to know the answers for everything and they will come, I promise. If we have to explain it or if you remember. But right now, we have to get somewhere safe first. Okay?"

She didn't give Eden a chance to respond before she spun around, her wild hair flinging around as she went. She ran down the stairs to the basement, calling, "Hurry, you two!"

They stepped into a room smaller than the lobby. The walls could have been sandstone, but Kai didn't trust himself enough to be sure. Steel doors broke up the brickwork while plumbing pipes and air vents lined the ceiling.

A few meters down, standing by a door with a

splash of white paint on it, Deacon was waiting. The door swung open, and a woman stepped through. Kai stared at her long hair, platinum blond with a splattering of black streaks. Going by what he knew about age, she looked to be early twenties. The woman rushed past Deacon straight for Zahra, there was a slight hiss in her tone as she asked, "Did you find them?"

"Just one," Zahra replied sadly, glancing over her shoulder.

Annika noticed Kai then, and she didn't try to hide her disdain. Scowling, she let her eyes wander to Eden beside him. She let out a huff. "Of course, you find Eden, but not Harper—Oh no—" her voice faded out as her gaze danced over his darkened head of hair. She stepped familiarly close and threaded her fingers through his tendrils, as though searching for pieces of him that were buried.

Gasping, she stepped back, tears in her eyes. "They got to Harper, too. Didn't they?"

"We don't know that," Zahra tried to placate.

"Ah, the rebellion has returned. You both must be happy to be back together again." A man walked through the opened door. He was tall and muscular. A dark beard with white patches covered his chin and his short hair matched. He stood beside the woman and put his hand on her shoulder, a tender squeeze.

Kai squinted as he took the sight in. Familiarity teased the edges of his mind. He knew this person. He admired this person.

"Wyatt?" he asked.

"Uhh..." Wyatt's brows fell then released. "Oh, what a relief, I saw no white in your hair and thought you—"

"He did," Zahra interrupted. "He just remembers a few things still."

Kai pointed at Wyatt, wagging his finger. "This guy." He turned to Eden, unable to contain his grin.

"He's the one who taught me how to drive."

Annika frowned, turning to Zahra. "How can he know that already?"

"One guess," Kobe said with a smirk, motioning his head in Eden's direction.

Wyatt threw his arms in the air, eyes lighting up. "Alistair's a genius."

"Alistair is an enabler," muttered Annika.

"You know my dad?" Eden piped. "Do you know where he is?"

One small sentence, that's all it took for Kai to want to wrap her in his arms, take her somewhere quiet, give her space to come to terms with it all. Instead, he moved his fingers across her palm and grasped her hand tight.

Wyatt's eyes hooded. "Sorry, no. But, if he is as kick-ass as he's always been, then I'd take a risk and say your dad will be perfectly fine."

Annika scoffed, a thin finger pointing in Eden's direction. "Heads-up. He's not your dad. He's someone who spends all his time acquiring things that are special and you just happen to be his pet project of the century."

"Wow," Kobe chided. "That's cruel, Annika, even for you."

"Yeah," Zahra added. "Everything he does is for the good of our people. This project to keep her from New Sanctuary during her restoration, it's worked just fine."

Annika's top lip curled. "She hasn't remembered everything yet; we'll see how well it worked. He's still an enabler if you ask me. What about us, fighting alone? He's protecting the wrong people, for the wrong reasons."

Kai felt his blood boil. This person spoke to Eden in such a way, it was almost as if she wanted to hurt her. He was about to shut her down when he felt Eden tense beside him.

She pulled her hand from his grasp, stepped forward, and scowled. "Listen, I know he's not my biological father, but he's been my dad for the last six years. You don't have to like him, but I just dare you to say one more nasty thing about him to me. Just try it."

Giving a smile not meant for anyone, Annika spun around and as she walked off, she said, "Welcome home, Eden."

"Annnyyy way," Wyatt boomed, slapping his hand on Eden's shoulder. "It's a great thing you're home. Kai hasn't shut up about you since he got his memories back a couple weeks ago... Well, before he lost them again."

Eden whipped her head in Kai's direction.

This time, it was his face that heated. "I, uhh... I don't remember that. But I guess it's probably true."

"It is true," Wyatt said, giving a teasing wink to Kai. "So, Eden, have you got your powers back yet?"

"Yes... umm, I can move things... with my thoughts," she replied.

Wyatt nodded as though he already knew. "That makes us cousins."

"I don't know what that means, but okay, cuz."

Wyatt chuckled quickly, then let out a long sigh. "You haven't changed a bit, Eeds. Having those powers means you're Azrael's descendant, like me."

"Azrael?" Eden craned her neck to Kai.

He couldn't help her though. He knew there were different Archangels for different abilities, but that's as far as he got. Shrugging, he mouthed, "Sorry."

"The Angel of Death." Annika leaned against the brick wall, picking at her nails. She seemed pleased to be the one sharing that information.

"But it's not like that," Wyatt was quick to add. "Azrael aids the transition from Earth to Heaven. We can create portals. Here, like this."

He swiveled around and held his arm out straight.

Mere inches from his fingertips, fragments of purple light appeared and a second later, they burst open, creating an opening about the size of a watermelon. Inside the portal, Kai could see Deacon, closer. Peering around, Kai found another purple-edged circle, hovering in front of Deacon.

Eden whispered, "That's not what I can do."

"Don't worry," Wyatt said, snapping his fingers, closing the portal. "After your powers come back, your full memory isn't too far behind."

Eden nodded and sent a shy eye to Kai.

"Wyatt?" Deacon called, wiping his lip where his wound was. "They're asking for dinner."

As Wyatt ran back through the door, Zahra squeezed herself between Eden and Kai. She looped her arms through theirs. "I bet you're starving. Food's this way."

"No!" Annika blurted. She pushed off the wall, one hand raised in Kai's direction. "Not you. Just because everyone else has forgiven you, doesn't mean I have. I've spent way too long protecting our kind, our children. And you screw it all up in one day... again. No, no way. You need to find Harper before she's killed."

"Annie," Zahra protested.

"Don't Annie me, Zah. You know what he did, you know what's at stake. He finds Harper or dies trying. I don't care at this point."

Swallowing, Kai's eyes twitched as he searched the floor. This person wasn't just angry for nothing. She was mad at him for something *he* did. Guilt flooded him, for God knows what. "I'm sorry," he whispered.

"What?" Annika snapped, death in her stare.

"I'm sorry," Kai said louder, looking up. "For whatever it was I did to you, to everyone. I'm sorry."

Annika's stare softened enough for a hint of forgiveness to seep through. She shook her head as though shaking the feeling off. "When you remember what you've done, you'll understand my disappointment."

Kai watched the woman stomp to the door and huff. "Deacon don't let them in. He can only enter New Sanctuary when he has Harper."

Deacon gave a curt nod. "Copy that, ma'am."

"Don't... ugh..." Annika lowered her voice, "Don't call me ma'am."

As she passed, he smirked. The first smile he'd given all night, and it was full of mischief. Kai realized then, that he and Deacon must have been friends.

"Don't worry about your sister, Kai, she's just upset because you left without waiting for her orders," Zahra said, looping her arm back through Eden's and dragging her toward the door.

"My sister?" Kai asked, hurrying to keep up.

"No." Kobe frowned, ignoring Kai. "She's upset because he took Harper with him."

"Yeah, that's what people say, but that's not the Kai I know." Zahra threw a thumb over her shoulder. "Is it the Kai you know?"

Kai glared at Kobe, all six feet of him, wondering who he was that they all knew. Kobe clenched his jaw and glanced at Kai. A smile flashed followed by a slight shake of his head. "No."

"The Kai I know," Deacon jibed, standing in front of the door with his arms crossed. "He wouldn't let his little sister out of those walls. I mean, he's done some pretty knuckle-headed things, but nothing like that."

It was a relief, to hear them speak of him that way. But there were still a few things that were hazy. Kai cleared his throat.

"Hey! Yeah, I'm right here guys," he said, waving. "That girl, Annika, she's my sister? Harper's my sister, too? And she's missing because of me? That's why Annika was being so cold to me?"

Kobe nodded. "Yup, that pretty much sums it up."

"Except for the part why Annika is cold to you,"

Deacon said.

"Hush, boy." Zahra waved a dismissive hand at Deacon. "Let him process the information he's just been bombarded with. He doesn't need to worry about anything else right now."

"What does she look like?" Eden asked, her eyes looking wider by the minute. "Harper."

Zahra laughed. "Like Annika but smaller, a little feistier too. And she's a pure."

"A pure?" Eden looked confused.

"Untouched by—" Kobe started.

"Her hair is pure white," Kai interrupted, knowledge hitting him like hail on a sunny day. "The same as Deacon's. They haven't lost their grace, ever."

From his spot by the door, Deacon looked over at Kai. His eyes narrowed as his chin lifted, almost proud at the recognition.

"Yes," Zahra said, excited. "You remember her?"

Kai took Eden's hand. A different kind of guilt crashed through him. Guilt that Eden was more in his mind than his own sister. He winced as he replied, "No, sorry."

He remembered one thing though. Pures were rare. When they were taken, and their grace and memories were drained, a little part of their hair became tainted forever. While it took years for their memories and abilities to return, their hair never did. It's how you knew how many times a Nephilim had been taken. By their hair.

Three times. Kai knew then. His grace had been taken three times.

16

Eden

Everyone knew Eden. And everyone acted like everything they were going through was normal.

Hunters chasing you in your home? Just a minor blip in the day.

You've got weird-ass powers? Yeah, me too, aren't we great?

You have no idea what I'm talking about? Don't worry, you will soon.

Eden sighed, staring at the four teens in front of her. Kai, the robot, who remembered things at a phenomenal rate. Being near him made her feel good, but also afraid, like he would take her down a path she'd never been before. Zahra, her long-time friend, who was a freaking werewolf. Zahra's twin, Kobe, who relaxed her, even without meaning to. And some boy named Deacon, who seemed to both hate and love everyone.

They knew her. Well. But as she waited for her

memories to return, she also felt like she was waiting for something else to drop.

Did she want to remember everything? There seemed to be so much she didn't know. Wyatt called them the rebellious two. And what did Kai mean when he said they were the reason for the curfew? They as in all the Nephilim, or they as in just the two of them? And why was Nephilim grace such a hot commodity?

She rested her head onto Zahra's shoulder, all at once tired. Zahra tugged her in close and shuffled for the now closed door. "Come on, guys, let's get them settled."

"I second that," Kobe said. "Let's eat. I'm always starving after a shift."

Deacon stood in front of them, arms crossed, and sniffed. "You heard the boss; *he* has to find Harper first."

Kobe looked down his nose. "Seriously, Deacon? All this time and you're doing what Annie says now?" Kobe moved in close and draped an arm over Deacon's neck. Pointing to Kai, he said, "Look at this guy. You can't tell me this time last week you weren't hanging off every word he was saying?"

Deacon eyed Kai. Then huffed. "Fine."

He rapped his knuckles on the door. One knock. Two knocks. Three fast taps. Then, he grabbed the handle and pulled the door wide open.

The room inside was a janitor's closet. A broom. A rubbish trolley. A few paint buckets.

Eden frowned staring into the small space. She rubbed her temples, trying to circle the sudden headache away. In the back corner, right beside a mop, a flicker of purple light swirled.

"Ugh," Deacon moaned, stepping inside. He leaned closer to the light and lifted his hand, pinching two fingers together. As soon as he touched the light, he separated his fingers.

The purple fragment burst open. A tiny dot

exploding into a wide circle the size of a door. The middle of the room changed from a closet to a grandiose dining room, about ten times the size of Eden's whole apartment.

Long tables made out of rustic logs lined the hall in three rows. Each table was filled with roast meats and baked potatoes and steamed vegetables, with tubs of various sauces between every pot. People chowed down on the food, oblivious to the portal.

Wyatt sat at the closest table, shoveling peas into his mouth. Deacon went through first, plonking himself on a table with no one at it. Kobe quickly followed, filling up his plate with goodies. Zahra stood in the middle of the portal waving her arm through.

"Come on," she said with a wide grin. "Before the food gets cold."

Kai stepped through, tugging gently on Eden's hand to follow. She complied. As soon as she was through, Wyatt gave a side smile and twisted his hand above his head. The portal closed behind them. A tiny purple flutter lingered in the air before disappearing completely.

The room was even better once inside. Strange yet familiar. Eden let her widened eyes wander the room, taking in all she could. It felt like she hadn't blinked in hours. Tea-light chandeliers hung from wooden beams on the roof. Flowers and plants hugged the corner beams, reaching around in natural decoration. Green and pink and purple.

Then, it happened. One by one the eyes landed on her. And by the time Zahra sat down and she was the only one left standing, everyone was staring, whispers filling the space around them.

"Welcome to New Sanctuary," Zahra said happily, scooping a pile of potatoes onto a plate. She placed it in front of Eden, then took a plate for herself.

Eden placed her backpack on the floor and sat down. She couldn't think about eating though, she was too busy studying the faces of everyone in the room. Some of them glared back, not so welcoming her eyes on them. And others, waved gleefully, almost with a hope that she knew them, too. She didn't though, nobody clicked. Not like Kai's face had.

One thing she did notice though, was the platinum hair. Some of them were like Annika, mostly white with streaks of brown. Some were like her and Wyatt, mostly brown with a line of silver. Kai was the only one without any white... except for a couple who had obvious dye colors splattered through their hair. Eden looked between Zahra and Kobe.

"You've dyed your hair?" Eden said, tucking her strand behind her ear.

The question made Kobe raise his scarred eyebrow, and he stroked his hair just above his ear. Zahra stopped mid-bite and glanced at her twin before looking at Eden. She nodded. "We wanted to blend in, while we watched over you."

"Watched over?" Eden frowned. "I thought we were friends?"

"Oh, yes, yes, of course," Zahra rushed. "We've always been friends. That's why they thought it was a good idea we lived close. So you could grow up with us."

Kobe reached his arm across the table and placed his hand close to Eden's. With a proud smile, he said, "It was my idea, actually. If you couldn't be near Kai, you may as well have us."

"Wait? If she couldn't be near me? They separated us?" Kai asked, mouth full of potato.

"The terrible two," Deacon muttered, stabbing peas. "As if they could keep you apart."

Zahra sat up straight and leaned forward to whisper. "They underestimate us though. It should really be the terrible five."

The glares from half the room made sense then. She'd done something they didn't agree with... *they'd* done something. Eden felt a familiar pang of guilt, even though she didn't know what it was she should be guilty of. Kai's words rang through her mind—*we're the reason for the curfew.* She looked at each face again. They all seemed to know her but she just couldn't...

She rolled her shoulders, trying to knead out the constant ache in her back. Staring at people wasn't going to bring her memories back. She'd looked at Zahra and Kobe every day for the last six years and nothing sparked. Kai was right though; the feeling always preceded the memory. And she felt... completely and utterly at home.

"Are you okay?" Zahra asked, eyebrows deepening in concern.

"I've been here before."

"Yes," Zahra replied. She bit her lip as though wondering what else to say. "It will all come back, trust me."

Eden nodded, satisfied. That was all she needed to know. Her memory was going to return, they'd all said it, they were all expecting it. And going by the peace she felt in that room, surrounded by people just like her, maybe getting her memories back wasn't going to be a bad thing after all. She cracked then, the edges of her mouth lifted, a smile breaking through. She scooped her fork under a pile of mashed pumpkin and began eating. A meal a thousand times better than a peanut butter and jelly sandwich.

After they'd devoured all the food from the table, the five sat in silence, Eden, still desperately trying to remember anyone or anything. Everyone had stopped staring at her, save a few sly glances every now and then.

Unable to contain the torment she broke the quiet. "I know I've been here before but I can't remember anything."

"Me too." Kai sighed and rested his elbows on the

table. "Well, parts. Like Wyatt teaching me to drive here. And a lake? There's a lake close by."

Deacon scoffed. "If you could call it that. More like a watering hole."

People began rising from their tables, taking their plates to the end of the hall. Annika walked past without uttering a word, her eyes piercing through Deacon. He watched her the whole way, and without smiling gave a slight shrug, as if to say *I am me and I do what I want.* When she was out of earshot, a smirk grew. He turned to Kai. "She's gotta be so pissed that you remembered Wyatt before her, too."

Kai laughed, looking at Deacon. "It's just so obvious you're a descendant of Chamuel, full of such positivity and light."

Eden forced her mouth shut. She didn't even know it had dropped open. Kai was remembering things at such a quick rate; she couldn't keep up. She'd been patient for the best part of six years, and now on the verge of everything she'd ever wanted to know, she could hardly bear it. She wanted to know more; she needed to know more, yet there he was filling in his own blanks.

Deacon's smile faded. He lowered his brows, eyes boring through Kai. In that moment, Eden wondered what kind of thing happened to a Nephilim to make them so standoffish and cranky all the time. But then, Deacon's eyes lit up and a hearty laugh boomed out. He whacked Kai's bicep. "Yeah? Good one, buddy."

Kobe grinned endearingly at Deacon. "He *is* an enigma."

Eden tried to contain her own laugh. Something about this moment with the four of them made her feel so light. So free. So at home.

"So, you can remember the Archangels and their gifts?" Zahra asked Kai.

He thought for a moment, then smiled as though surprised. "Yeah, I guess I do."

Eden was happy for him. Truly. No amount of jealousy lived inside her. Because soon she would be remembering similar things.

Zahra pointed at Eden. "Your dad *is* a genius. This serum he created; it changes everything."

New Sanctuary, Eden had learned, was exactly as the name implied. A hideout. A place they could be Nephilim without the fear of being hunted. A few people stayed there, never leaving its sheltered space. A few, like Zahra and Kobe, ventured in and out of the real world, doing all they could to protect their kind.

While others, like herself, became stuck in a cycle. Captured, grace taken, no memory, repeat. This time was different though, she didn't want to get captured again.

After dinner, Deacon had disappeared with Kobe, and Zahra led Kai and Eden out of the food hall. She took them outside. Night had fallen but only just, the last flicker of sunlight dipping below a mountain. Eden realized they weren't near New York anymore.

From the outside, Eden could see that the food hall was a renovated barn, sitting on an expansive lush field in a valley. Forest surrounded them on three sides, and the fourth had long cornstalks, swaying in the breeze. Mountains reached above them, snow topping their rocky peaks. Yes, she'd definitely been there before.

Zahra led them to an identical barn a few yards from the first. As Eden stepped inside, her heart leapt. Countless mats were rolled out on the floor, covered with sleeping bags and pillows. The main part of the barn was a little smaller than the food hall, and at the end there were extra rooms with bathroom and toilet symbols on their doors. A ladder reached up to a U-shaped mezzanine, where sofas and beanbags filled out the space, and books rested on small shelves along the wall.

"The living room," Zahra said, sweeping her arm in a semi-circle showcasing the area.

Kai looked around and pointed to a mat in the top corner, slightly separated from the rest. "That's mine."

"I'll be back," Zahra said, rushing off.

Glancing around the room, Eden started counting all the makeshift beds. There weren't any more than thirty. Surely, there were more Nephilim than that.

"We're refugees," Kai stated.

Turning to face him, she found him giving her a sad smile. He seemed different from what he had been when he walked into her living room half-naked, with no memory of his own. Less innocent and naïve, more aware and experienced. She asked, "Do you remember?"

His brow fell. "Parts. It's hard to grasp. I remember things as they present themselves. Like, I wouldn't have been able to remember this room but when I walked in here, I knew what it was, why we were here, where I slept."

"Do you remember why you left us?" Kobe asked from behind them.

"I..." Kai's frown deepened. He reached over his shoulder, digging his fingers into his shoulder blade. "I left you?"

"Yeah, a week ago, right after your full memory returned. You just up and left. Took Harper... or so Annika thinks."

Kai dropped his hand to his side and looked around the room. He returned his gaze to Eden. Her heart sped up as she watched him think, as she watched him remember.

With his eyes still on Eden, he said, "I left for *her*. Everyone was talking about Eden getting her memories back, too. I knew she'd get her powers first, like the time before... I didn't want the Hunters to catch her again."

Kobe chuckled. "And you got caught instead?"

"I guess I did." Kai shrugged, taking Eden's hand, his aqua-blues boring into her soul.

"You knew we were with her, right? She didn't need protecting."

"I know," Kai answered, still staring at Eden. He spoke as if she wasn't there. But, even with Kobe right beside them, she felt as if they were the only two people in the room. "I couldn't stay away any longer. When my own memory returned, the time before this, well, six years without her was enough."

"Where do you want this?" Zahra bumped into Eden with a rolled-up mat in her arms. She pointed across the back wall, to the middle bed in the row. "Next to me?"

Eden let her eyes wander down the row to an unmade mat beside Zahra's. The next mat along was occupied by Deacon, lying on his back with his hands under his head, staring at the ceiling. In between Deacon and Kai's bed in the corner, there was an unoccupied space the perfect size for a mat. Feeling Kai's smooth palm press against her, she squeezed, not wanting to let go.

"Or near Kai?" Zahra said less enthused.

"Stop teasing the poor girl and put her next to Kai." Kobe ripped the mat out of Zahra's hands and started walking to the corner. He looked over his shoulder and teased, "You can't compete with the terrible two."

"I'm not trying to compete," she yelled at her brother's back. She turned back to Eden. "And you're not so much terrible... but trouble does follow you when you're together. It's why they tried separating you both." She smacked her lips together and raised her eyebrows. "But, here we are."

A sentence like that should have hurt. But it wasn't the words that Eden heard, it was the intent.

And she knew within her soul, that whatever she and Kai did in the past, Zahra, Kobe, and probably even Deacon, were all right there alongside them.

Zahra sighed and glanced down at Eden gripping onto Kai. She rolled her eyes and sighed again. "Even amnesia can't keep you two apart."

Eden felt blood rush to her face and promptly snatched her hand free. She hadn't realized how tightly she was holding on. Everyone seemed to believe the two of them had some kind of unbreakable bond. She barely knew him. Sure, they'd been on the run for two days and she'd not wanted to leave his side since the moment she saw him...

She hated herself for it. He wasn't a robot, she never actually believed that he could have been. But it would have been easier if he was. Somewhere deep inside her being, she knew that letting herself get close to him was dangerous. Not that she would lose herself, no, it was that she could find herself. Every small part of her that was missing was hidden inside him. And that scared her. Because the pain she felt looking at him behind glass, she never wanted to feel that again.

Regardless, she let the twins set her mat up next to Kai's. Because no matter how scared she felt, there was nowhere else she'd rather be.

"We'll give you some time to process," Zahra said, stepping back.

"See you in the morn," Kobe said, tapping his index finger to his forehead.

Eden sat down on the mattress, so thin she could feel the coolness of the cement beneath it. She looked around the room. Most people had stopped staring at her, but every now and then the odd one would rush a glance their way.

Kai sprawled over his mattress; arms propped behind him. He was looking around the room, too. His gaze would rest on certain people, sometimes his eyes would light up with recognition and other times they would hood over and a small crease would form between his brows as if the expression could make him remember them.

"Hey, Robot?" Eden asked lightly.

Kai glared at her and leaned forward, resting his elbows on his bent knees. He turned his cheek as if refusing to answer to that name.

Eden proceeded anyway. "Tell me more."

"About what?" Kai inched forward; any hint of annoyance gone.

"All these people... the Nephilim, have we always slept on floors?"

Kai chewed on his bottom lip. "No. It's not our real home. Our real home... It's hazy. An ambush, I think."

"By the Hunters?"

A sparkle hit his eyes. A new memory reaching through the mud. As soon as the recollection came, his face dropped. "Yes." He grazed his thumb over his full lips, thinking, remembering. "They came for us when we were young."

"Twelve?"

"Younger." Kai dropped his hand, and it landed on her bare foot. "Six."

"Six? Why?" She knew the answer for that. "Our grace?"

Kai nodded. "Mm-hmm. They took us for our grace. And in the process, they made us forget."

Eden rested her chin on her shoulder as she scanned the room once more. All these people, scared and in hiding, hoping to remember their yesterdays. "They still come for us?"

"Every six years, when our powers return."

"Just so you know," a voice beside them interrupted. Deacon rolled up; eyes low. "The people here? This is a drop in the pond of how many Nephilim there used to be."

He rolled back down again.

Kai's eyes flitted between Eden's, and as if speaking while the memories came, he said, "Oh God, Eden. They have so many of us there right now. Hundreds, no, thousands. That's if they're still alive."

A burning sensation circled in Eden's stomach. Fire rising from within. "Well, we have to do something. We have to find them, save them. Stop this madness."

Kai nodded, fists tightening together.

Ever so quietly, a small chuckle came from Deacon's direction. With his eyes closed, he said, "Oh, you two. That's what you always say."

Eden

Eden stirred in her sleep. Neurons fired across her mind, like a cascade of fireworks lit in succession. Another memory.

One of a lake. A green-tinged-blue lake. And a kayak.

The water matched his eyes.

They were celebrating something. The two of them had just shown themselves to the world, an attempt at opening humans' eyes to their presence. She felt unstoppable with him by her side...

Eden dipped her fingers into the still water. It was chilled, as though the ice had only just melted. "We did the right thing."

"I know."

Behind her, Kai kicked up his heels. He leaned back in their kayak and with his hands behind his head; he lifted his face to the sky. Stars spotted across the darkness, a twinkle of hope.

Eden sighed and twisted around. "What do you think the others will say?"

"Who cares?" Kai teased, an arrogant smile on his twelve-year-old face. "They weren't doing anything, so we had to."

As she nodded, Kai began rocking side to side. Eden flung her hands out, grasping the edges of the kayak. Her wings unfurled—black at their base, and white at the tips. They were like none other, two-toned and beautiful.

Kai laughed. With shaking legs he stood and his large wings reached out at his sides. Iridescent, blue feathers shimmered like pearls in the moonlight. A teasing glimmer flashed across his eyes as he continued the swaying movement.

Eden flapped her wings before the kayak toppled upside down. Her toes skimmed the water, and she grinned. "Watch out, Malakai, you don't want to mess with me."

Kai hovered in the air, watching Eden as she rose to meet him. "Oh yeah? I'm a Warrior Angel, remember?"

"You won't let me forget." She poked her tongue out as she used her powers to pull him down to her level.

"That's not fair," he said, pouting. Then, the corners of his lips lifted and he pressed his hands on her shoulders.

He pushed hard, sending her backward. She tumbled through the wind, stopping herself before she hit a tree.

"Oh, that's it," Eden threatened. She brought her wings down and up and then down, picking up momentum as she sped toward him.

He didn't move. Just stayed there in midair, smiling. Waiting.

"Hey!" A man's voice echoed across the lake. He was standing on the jetty in front of the chateau. He had something in his hand, a gun maybe.

"That's our cue to go," Kai said. He reached for Eden an easy laugh tumbling through his lips.

As she moved closer to him, the man below called, "Demons! I found the demons."

"Demon?" Eden stopped mid-flight.

Kai stopped laughing, a frown falling. "How insulting."

The man on the jetty raised his weapon. It wasn't a normal gun. It was a spear gun. The noise it made as it hurtled for them was like a whip cracking in the wind. Eden watched as it fell short of them, landing in the water. The man muttered to himself and reeled the weapon in.

Kai smirked. "Humans are funn—"

A harpoon pierced through Kai's wing and body, the arrow's tip settling on the front side of his shoulder. The child-like smirk dropped and a cry of pain bellowed from deep within. He threw his hand straight to his shoulder where blood poured down his shirt, soaking it in lines of crimson. Behind him, his wing was caught, and he struggled to stay afloat with one wing.

Eden screamed at the sight. Heart thumping against her rib cage, she held her arm forward as she raced for him. She pulled at the harpoon with her mind, but it wouldn't budge. No matter how hard she tried, it felt like opposing ends of a magnet fighting for the right of way. "Something's wrong."

Kai clutched at the weapon and yanked, but even his super-strength couldn't break it. Grimacing, Kai studied the harpoon. It was made of silver and blackwood, laced in bronze swirls. "It's the dampener, like the clasps. We can't use our powers."

Blood oozed from around the arrowhead. Kai jolted and began moving toward the ground. The man began reeling him in.

Eden rushed to him, tears stinging her eyes, and

threw her arms around his neck.

"Let me go, Edie," Kai rasped. "There's no use in both of us going back there."

"Never." Eden buried her head in his shoulder and wrapped her legs around his waist.

Kai grabbed her ribs and tried to pry her off him, but he was weakened by blood loss and her grip was locked tight. He urged, "Eden. We've only just got our memories back."

She gripped tighter still. "Where you go, I go."

"Eden!" The closer to the ground they got, the more panicked Kai's voice became. "You need to let me go."

"Never."

A harpoon speared her side, right above her hip.

The pain seared, and she sprung up. Wide awake, back in the present, Eden clutched at her side. Her lungs pumped rapidly as she tried to catch her breath. She scrunched the bottom of her shirt in a fist, lifted it to just under her breast, and smoothed her palm over the small scar that remained.

"Are you all right?" Kai whispered, sitting up.

Startled, she dropped her shirt, but under his kind expression, she softened. Eden shuffled over, grabbed at the collar of his top, and pulled it down as far as it could stretch. A raised, light-purple scar, curved around his shoulder. She stared at it for a moment, feeling his eyes on her.

One breath.

She'd have to admit it.

Another breath.

She'd have to accept it.

The memories of Kai weren't so distant anymore. Being around him felt natural, as innate as breathing air. It was in that moment she realized she'd stopped seeing him as a stranger. He was real and beside her. He was a person. Her person.

She let go of his top and met his gaze. "Kai?"

"You remember?"

"I remember."

She fell forward, collapsing her whole body against his. Her arms bent around his neck as she let the tears fall. His strong hands hovered at her back for a moment before bearing down. He slid his arms around her, squeezing her tight.

She was home. Safe. Loved.

18

Kai

Kai decided that memories brought pain.

Droplets of hot water cascaded over his body. He stood in the shower, hanging his head, hands pressed against the tiles to support himself. Eden wasn't the only one who'd remembered things overnight. Visions of his long-forgotten past careened through his mind on a loop. Snippets that he'd caught over the last few days turned into a whole. Eighteen full years.

What he wouldn't do to rewind a day, to be with Eden in that sweet bliss of knowing her and no other. But then, he thought of Harper. Her bright blue eyes and long platinum locks. Her mischievous laugh and cocksure attitude. That fourteen-year-old had his heart, too, and she was missing because of his recklessness.

He thumped his knuckles into the shower wall and cracked a tile. A trickle of blood ran down his finger and he watched it pour. It won't heal, he told himself.

Guilt did that. And shame. His body could survive bullets and knives and anything that would render a human lifeless but guilt prolonged healing and left scars to remind him of his failures. He lifted his hand to the front of his shoulder, wiping the blood over the raised scar. A simple harpoon gave it to him, but his sadness made the wound remain.

Eden had just remembered that awful time of being captured for the second time, just before they were taken to the extraction chambers where their grace was removed. They were put into glass cages and tubes were inserted into their veins. Eden's grace was extracted first. He was forced to watch as all her life as she knew it disappeared from her eyes. They were kept in smaller steel cages afterward, shells of themselves, not even knowing how to speak.

She was also the first to be saved. As the Hunters opened her cage and dragged her away, her frail body and confused eyes searched for something familiar. They fell on him, but she didn't recognize him, just as he didn't recognize her. He didn't know until his memory returned six years later, who she was and that she was traded. Alistair somehow found a way to obtain her. A handful of others were saved too, including himself, and taken back to New Sanctuary.

Hundreds were still there though. Every six years, their grace returned, only to be sucked dry again. He didn't have to remain in a steel cage to know what that felt like.

Their full memory returned. They suddenly realized who they were and what they could do. Then, it was taken again, and the whole cycle of torture began once more.

Kai turned the faucet off and stepped out of the shower. With steam swirling around him, he sighed and grabbed a towel. There was no way he could stay in New Sanctuary, not while knowing the horrors of extraction. He decided then, that he'd do anything to get them back.

Wrapping a towel around his waist, he chuckled to himself. That's what he'd thought before too, when he and Eden were twelve and their memories returned. They told each other their actions were for justice, while everyone just called them rebellious.

"How'd you sleep?" Zahra asked as Kai sat down at the table.

"As good as can be expected," Kai replied. He cast an eye on Eden, knowing hers was the answer Zahra was truly interested in.

Eden was mid-strawberry-chew. She swallowed and grinned. "Best night ever. I remember what happened at Lake Louise. And New York."

Deacon practically threw his bowl of oats on the table and slumped next to Eden. "I wouldn't go declaring that to everyone."

"Yes. Well, we were twelve and wanted to do something instead of sitting around here singing kumbaya," Eden returned fire.

Kai held in a laugh. She was fitting right back into life at New Sanctuary, as though she'd always been there like he wished she had.

Deacon raised his brow and swung his head in her direction. He let his eyes dance around her face before nodding in approval. "I didn't say I thought it was a bad choice." He waved a spoon in her direction. "But it's nice to have the feisty you back, Eeds."

"How about you, Kai? Any more memories?" Zahra turned her attention.

Kai dropped his eyes to his cereal and tapped his spoon on the edge of the bowl. He contemplated a lie to save Eden's feelings. But then opted for the truth, because that's what she deserved.

"Everything," he said to his bowl. "I remember it all."

He felt Eden stiffen beside him.

"So where's Harper, then?"

Kai twisted in his seat to find Annika hunched over the end of the table, fingers sprawling against the wooden panels. She stared at him, waiting. And Kai understood why she was so angry at him, why she hated him.

His actions caused widespread panic. The humans, the innocent ones, they saw him and Eden fly through New York, but they didn't see Nephilim that needed saving, they saw demons who wanted to hurt them. And the other humans, the exploitative ones, used that fear to create the curfew. It was their guise to hunt Nephilim while the whole world slept. His actions didn't just cause panic, they made it easier for his own people to be taken.

Not only that though. She didn't hate him for that. She hated him for other reasons, too. Things he wasn't quite ready to accept yet.

Kai looked at his sister in the eyes, unwilling to yield to her threatening stance. "I don't know where she is."

His older sister scowled. "I swear to God, Kai. If she's..." Annika halted. Her words caught in her breath. She turned away, wincing. After a long sigh, she turned back, recomposed. "I'll send you to your death. Do you hear me?"

The cool steel of the spoon's handle indented into Kai's tightening fist. The heat of rage rose within. It took only a second for him to stand and tower over her. "If anything happens to her, I'll send myself to death."

A collective gasp echoed around the food hall. It wasn't the first time the two of them went toe to toe. Normally though, it was about the past. This time felt different, as though the future hung in the balance.

Kai knew it. He'd screwed up. He didn't know Eden was safe with Alistair; he thought she was lost and alone, or worse. He'd ranted too much about saving her. And Harper at fourteen years old was impressionable. She'd wanted to leave with him, determined to save her brother's kindred spirit. His answer of no, it wasn't enough though. He didn't know why he thought it would be enough—that he could just tell her she wasn't going with him and she'd be okay with that. Of course, she wouldn't.

Annika stood her ground. She wasn't that much shorter than him and she'd beaten him in practice countless times. Kai resigned. Both his sisters were stubborn.

He took a step back, shoulders hunching in submission. "I'll find her, I promise."

"You're not going anywhere, brother," Annika spat. "Leave it to adults to clean up your mess." Her eyes flitted to Eden. "You'll spend the day training before you go and do something that will get your mind wiped for good."

"What? No. I'm going out again, I have to find her," Kai protested.

The warmth of blood soaring through his veins was torture. Annika wasn't the boss of him. There was no way he'd stay there and do nothing. He never had. He never would.

"Enough," Annika yelled, sending the whole room to silence. She lowered her head, eyes as fierce as the sun. Through gritted teeth, she said, "Just once, Kai. Do as you're told."

Kai swallowed his anger, but it didn't go far. It sat in his throat like a lump, waiting in anticipation for the perfect moment. He knew his sister didn't trust him. But she didn't realize that he was older... he was wiser. He wasn't just going to fly through a city and expect change. No, this time he'd do it properly. He'd take the whole operation down. He was going to save all the Nephilim and make sure it would never happen again.

"Malakai?" Annika hissed. "You're not going

anywhere; do you understand me?"

Kai blinked and met his sister's glare. It almost killed him to say it. A whisper came out. "I understand."

Annika nodded once, satisfied. She ran a judgmental eye over Eden as she walked away. Kai swallowed again, anger bubbling on simmer.

"Jeez," Deacon said, shoveling oats into his mouth. "You've really done it this time."

"Shut-up, Deac," Kai mumbled, falling onto his chair.

He hated to admit it but Annika was right. He couldn't leave, not yet. Eden would want to help him; she'd be so pissed if he went without her. But he couldn't drag her into a war right now, not like this. She didn't even have all her memories back. Ugh, that damn sister was right. They needed to train.

19

Eden

Twenty children and teenagers stood in a line out on the field. Six leaders faced them, one to represent each Archangel.

Eden had learned a little bit about what each group was and what they could do. She was still unsure whether she really was the same as Wyatt though. She had telekinesis, not teleportation. But then, none of the other groups had telekinesis as their power either.

"You've got me today, Roses," said a woman with white hair that fell to her waist. She smiled brightly as her pale-pink wings with rose-gold edges unfurled, and she flew like a bolt of lightning toward the cornfield.

"Come on, jerks," Deacon jibed, following her. Seven kids between the ages of three and fifteen, chased after him, smiling wider than the Cheshire cat.

Oh, there's the Chamuel positivity and light that seemed to have skipped Deacon, Eden thought, looking at their bright faces.

Next in the line, was a woman similar in age to Annika. Her hair was cut short and a thick line of black locks framed her face. Zahra said her name was Lucinda, her mentor and cousin. They were descendants of Ariel, the Archangel of Animals, and had the power to shape-shift into any animal they desired. Lucinda rolled her neck around, dropped to her knees, and transformed into a leopard. Leaping from her hind legs, she sped into the forest. Zahra and Kobe laughed, and as they ran after her, they both shifted—Zahra into a dove, and Kobe, a horse.

An older woman with green eyes, the only elder Eden had noticed, stepped forward. Her white loose curls, bounced against her radiant face as she stepped into the crowd of those who were left. As she passed on through, she collected four young children and kept walking to the food hall silently. Healers, Zahra had told Eden. Born of Raphael.

There was only Eden, Kai, and five others remaining.

"Jophiel's descendants," said a man around Wyatt's age with dark skin and bulging muscles. "What element shall we practice today?"

"Water please, Lionel," one child boomed.

"Fire!" another called, a hint of excitement in his eyes.

"We did fire yesterday," the first child whined.

"Yes," Lionel agreed. "Let's do water today."

He lifted off the ground, and large yellow wings moved gently above him. Four children followed him.

A girl about the age of sixteen peered around Kai and gawked at Eden. She had dark upturned eyes, tanned skin, and bright purple hair. She wore a baggy sweater that almost hit her knees. As she stared at Eden, her top lip rolled up. The look was peculiar and Eden couldn't decide whether she was frowning or just being curious.

"Eden, Jia, you're with me," Wyatt called, waving

them to him.

"Come on, brother," Annika sighed, turning around. She flung her head over her shoulder. "Oh, Jia, just a heads-up... she's not a normal Azrael descendant."

"What do you mean?" Jia scrunched her nose.

"Direct," Annika said, walking off. "Like us."

Kai dragged his feet, his hands balling in and out of fists, as he begrudgingly met up with his sister. Spinning around, he walked backward, eyes on Eden. He gave a quick wave as he mouthed the words, "Have fun."

"Jeez," Jia said, looking at Eden with a frown. "I'm surrounded by royalty."

"What the hell does direct mean?" Eden wondered out loud.

"A child," Wyatt answered. "Not grandchild or great-grandchild or four times great-grandchild like most of us. You're a freaking child. It means your powers are insanely strong. Just like Annika, Kai, and Harper. They are children of Michael. It's why Annika is our leader. No one wants to mess with that strength."

Eden glanced over her shoulder at Annika with Kai. They stood a meter apart, stance wide, fists clenched and raised. Is that what her dad meant when he said she was special?

"Okay, earth to Eden," Wyatt said, waving a hand in front of her face. "Training is important. I need your undivided attention."

"Yeah." Jia laughed, digging her elbow into Eden's ribs. "Just forget that Malakai, the lover boy, exists for this short moment in time, yeah?"

Eden blinked, blood rushing to her face. "He's... he's not my lover."

Wyatt nodded. "Good. I can't imagine any good will come from the son of a warrior and the daughter of death herself hooking up."

Resentment rushed through Eden's bones. Daughter of death sounded so dark... almost evil. Why couldn't she be something more benevolent, like a Healer or a Shield like Deacon?

"Anyway." Jia stretched her hand to Eden. "I'm Jia. And in case you didn't already gather, we've never met. Well, we have, but you were two years older than me and we were taken when we were practically infants, and I've only just been released back here, so I don't remember you. Well, I don't remember a lot of things. But anyway, hiya."

Eden stared at the girl in front of her. She had long straight hair—dyed purple mostly—but there were two lighter streaks down one side, as though the hair underneath was platinum. Going by the calculations of those lighter streaks, Jia's grace had been extracted twice. Just like Eden. And her memory was returning, just like Eden's.

"Don't leave the girl hanging," Wyatt teased.

Eden's eyes dropped to Jia's hand waiting between them. She ignored it and instead fell forward, draping her arms around her cousin. Jia froze under the hold for a moment before softening into the embrace.

When they parted, Eden watched a lone tear fall silently down Jia's face. "I've been alone for so long."

Eden couldn't imagine it. All those Nephilim, trapped inside cages for their whole lives. It was all they knew. Any resentment Eden had about her own memories and forgotten childhood, suddenly vaporized. And it was in that moment, Eden decided she was going to train her hardest to get a hold of her powers. Because she was the daughter of the Angel of Death and she needed to prepare for war.

"That's it, girl, you've got it," Wyatt encouraged.

Beads of sweat rolled off Jia's forehead as a small

portal the size of a basketball shimmered between her hands. She gasped for breath as she struggled to maintain it. Wyatt stood in front of her, bending over so their faces were level.

"Bigger," he ordered.

Jia let out a moan as she widened her hands. Knees wobbling together, she gasped, "I don't know how much longer I can hold it."

"Until it's large enough to walk through. Go bigger." Wyatt kicked Jia's feet farther apart. "Strengthen your stance."

Eden winced in sympathy. She stood back with her arms crossed and frowned, watching Jia battling to stay upright. For a nice guy, her cousin sure was a hard-ass.

An almighty cry tumbled out of Jia as she bent her knees and widened her arms. Black wings unraveled, almost too large for her small body. The portal opened, expanding twice the size it was. Through it, Eden could see the food hall and Raphael's Healers sat at a table cheering for Jia.

Almost as soon as the portal opened, it closed again. Jia's wings disappeared, and she collapsed to the ground, sobbing. "I did it."

"Not yet," Wyatt said, grasping her shoulder. "You need to remove the remnant."

Above Jia's head, a tiny flicker of purple remained. She lifted her hand and twisted it slightly. The remnant sparkled in a final flare and then vanished. Letting herself roll backward, Jia lay on the grass, arms wide, lungs pumping.

"A remnant," Wyatt said to Eden, pointing at the empty space, "is a potential doorway. You must always make sure to remove them."

Eden nodded, unsure if she'll even need to worry about it.

"I have a question." Jia propped herself up onto her elbows. "Why don't the Archangels come here and help us? All their children trapped in confinement and they are where? Playing hacky sack in Heaven?"

Wyatt balked. "Jesus, Jia, have some respect."

"Sorry," she replied softly.

"Anyway, they aren't like us. They lose their powers on Earth. It's why they created us, so we could live here and do what they can't. And no, they don't play hacky sack, they rule and observe. Okay..." Wyatt cracked his hands together. "Eden, your turn."

"Uhh..." Eden hesitated. It was a peculiar thing being told to do something she'd never done before. She didn't even know where to begin.

Wyatt passed Jia a drink and walked to Eden. "You want a rundown?"

Eden nodded.

"Set your feet strong below you, make sure you are anchored against the ground." Wyatt shuffled his heels into the soil, bending his knees slightly. He brought his hands together, fingertip to fingertip. "Put your hands like this, then think of a place. That's it."

Eden mimicked his movements. With her hands clasped together, she looked up. "That's it? Are you sure?"

Clearly amused, Wyatt unlocked her fingers. "Loosely together. And then, as you think of a place, separate your hands. Best to start off with somewhere in New Sanctuary."

"Right." Eden wasn't convinced. She looked at the cornfield and imagined herself there. One deep breath later she opened her hands. Nothing appeared between them. "I don't think I can do this."

Wyatt frowned. "I thought you said you had your powers back."

"I do." Eden let her hands fall to her sides. "But not those ones."

"Which... which ones?" Wyatt asked hesitantly.

Looking around, Eden spotted a strand of grass longer than the rest. She considered what she wanted to do with it, and a moment later, the blade of grass tore from the soil and floated into the air. Eden raised her hand, and the blade tumbled forward until it landed in her palm.

"Jeez," Jia said with sparkling eyes, still sitting on the ground. "When can I learn that?"

"You can't." Wyatt took the grass from Eden and held it in front of his face. "It's not something we can do."

"It's not?" Eden asked, confused. Didn't they just say she was a child of Azrael? What made her so different? "Is it to do with me being a direct child and not a descendant?"

Wyatt faced Eden but he couldn't look her in the eye. "Something like that."

"That doesn't sound like a definitive answer." Eden crossed her arms, wondering if Wyatt wasn't telling her something. "Why am I different?"

She watched Wyatt drop the grass and dust his hands off. He said, "One thing at a time, Eeds. Okay? Let's focus on the right here, right now. And right now, I need you to create me a portal."

Eden sighed. "You remind me of my dad you know? Evasive answers and half-truths."

"Thank you," Wyatt grinned. "Now practice."

Eden

"Do you think we could make a really big portal with four hands?" Jia asked, sitting cross-legged on the grass opposite Eden.

They'd finished their training and Wyatt had already left. It wasn't for lack of trying but Eden couldn't create a portal, not even a glimmer of light. She sat on the ground, picking at grass strands, her eyes drifting to the end of the field where Annika had taken Kai into the forest. The evergreen trees on that side of the field reached up a mountain whose peak was hidden behind wispy clouds. There were spiky branches and rocky cliffs, but no Kai or Annika.

"Maybe," Eden said, letting a handful of grass trickle from her grasp. "I wouldn't know."

"Aww, come on. Don't be upset. It took me four lessons to make my first fragment. You'll get there."

Eden didn't have the heart to tell Jia that wasn't what she was upset about. She was upset because all her teenage life she felt different, and now that she'd found her people, she still felt different. And still no closer to knowing herself fully.

There was so much that didn't make sense. Like, why were thirty Nephilim living in the woods instead of doing angelic things, like saving people... like saving their people?

She knew she tried to before, in a roundabout kind of way. She and Kai flew through New York because they wanted humans to understand they were real and that they needed help. How could anyone turn away from something they saw with their own eyes? It didn't quite work out the way the twelve-year-olds had planned it, but it'd been six years and still, no one had tried anything else. It almost felt like they were all too scared and that was odd to Eden because they were freaking Angels.

"Why don't we use our powers to portal to our people who are caged?" she mused.

"Our powers don't really work like that," Jia said, placing her fingertips together like a steeple. She pulled her hands apart, creating a tiny circle. Through it, Eden could see the edge of the forest. "First, you have to know where you're going, and then it only really works for places you know or can find on a map. Like, I can't go to my old cage, I wouldn't have the faintest idea where it is but if you pointed out a spot on a map, easy." A leopard stepped out of the forest in the center of Jia's portal, followed swiftly by a horse, and above them, a dove. Jia clapped her hands together, closing the portal. "Well, in theory. You're gonna want to be specific. Imagine opening a portal in a boys locker room or something?"

Eden gave a sad laugh. She liked Jia already, with her Asian eyes, soulful and eager, with her verbal diarrhea and all. It surprised her though, how someone with Jia's past could be the way she was. Both times Eden was extracted, she had been immediately traded back into the fold—the first, when she was six to New Sanctuary, and the second, when she was twelve to New York. It hardly seemed fair that

Jia didn't get the chance.

"How are you so positive? You've spent most of your life in a cage." Eden didn't mean for it to come out so harsh, but there it was, an honest question, lingering in the air between them.

Jia dropped her hands to her lap, took a sharp inhale, then through a toothy grin, she replied, "Because I'm not in one anymore."

Coming out of the forest, Zahra and Kobe shifted back into their human forms. They stormed past Eden and Jia in a straight line for the food hall. Kobe swiveled, and running backward, he shouted, "Sorry, can't stop. Too hungry."

Thwack.

The sound of fist to face sent sonic waves rippling across the sky above them. Eden saw Kai and Annika emerge through the cloud that surrounded the mountain. Wings out and muscles contracted, the two of them were at war. They clashed together and pulled apart, and Eden swore she almost saw a smile on Annika's face as she sped toward Kai like a flying spear.

"Oh my God." Eden jolted, ready to use her powers to pull Annika away.

Jia's hand quickly found Eden's shoulder. "No worry with them. They do this all the time."

Eden winced as Annika thumped Kai against the chest with her palm. The impact sent him tumbling into the forest behind the barn. His body cracked through tree branches on his fall to the ground.

"And that happens all the time, too." Jia cackled with glee.

Eden turned back around. "He's okay?"

"Yep. Listen, this is my observation, and I've only just arrived here, so take it however you like." Jia rested her elbows against her crossed knees, looking into the forest where Kai had fallen. "But when his memory was returning—before he got his full memory back and left to find you—his powers came first and he was out there with her fighting like this day and night. Any chance he got. It's weird though." She inched forward and spoke with a hushed voice as if she were telling a secret. "He's stronger than she is, everybody says it. But she always wins."

A chorus of giggles rolled across the field. Eden whipped her head to see Chamuel's descendants landing. All of them except Deacon.

Jia tilted her head, watching the row of bubbly Shields gallop for the barn. She craned her neck back to where they landed and seeing no one else there her shoulders slumped. Sighing, she turned back around. "Shield Angels are the best."

Eden fought the urge to ask if she had a thing for Deacon. "Oh yeah? How is that?"

Jia's dark brown eyes sparkled. "I've only just found this out and you're gonna love it as much as I do. Shield Angels have special feathers. They have this energy dampening thing in them... or a way to hide our signal... or..." Her brows lowered. "Well, I don't know how it works, but they've placed feathers together with black obsidian stones all around us in a five-mile radius, and bam, we're hidden in plain sight. That's why they're the best." Behind her, down near the cornfield, Deacon landed. Grinning, she twisted her body, and with a wistful tone said, "They're literally our heroes, keeping us safe from evil."

Her gaze followed Deacon. He sauntered for the barn, looking at his feet as he kicked tufts of grass along the way. Slapping her knees, Jia huffed, "Well, all this training makes me hungry, you coming?"

Smiling, Eden jumped to her feet and dusted her backside. "Sure."

They wandered to the food hall and made their way to the serving table, where Kai was, stacking his plate with three burgers. He had a small cut on his hairline and as Eden got closer, she noticed it heal, leaving blood but no scar. When he noticed Eden watching him, he gave an embarrassed smile.

"Fighting makes me hungry," he explained.

Eden helped herself to a burger from his plate. "Does it hurt?"

His eyes widened. "What?"

"When you fight? Does it hurt?" she said, before taking a bite.

Kai squinted, watching her eat. He glanced down at his plate and back up again. "That's... that's... mine —"

"How're you rat-cakes doing?" Deacon slid next to Kai, patting him on the back.

Beside Eden, Jia let out a tiny peep.

Ignoring Deacon, Kai stared at Eden. The look in his eyes sent her brain ticking. She'd seen that look before; it was long ago but here, right in this very place. As the sweet memory graced her mind, Kai gave a playful scowl. He covered his plate with a hand and shuffled to the closest table.

"Ahh, I see. You've made a rookie mistake," Deacon said. He took a burger from the serving tray and peeled the top bun off. Throwing the pickle back onto the tray, he continued, "You don't mess with that boy's food. It's all right, you'll remember."

Eden took a small bite out of the burger and with a mouth full of food, she said, "Oh, I remember. I just don't care." She caught a glimpse of Deacon's surprised face as she swiveled around.

As she slumped herself into the spot next to Kai, he gave her a bashful glance. In reply, she held out her half-eaten burger. "Want some?"

At first, he looked confused and then his face lit up. Eden knew that he understood she'd remembered something specific. A moment from when they were younger.

She'd always share her food with him, with anyone, but he'd never offer the same in return. He'd guard his food as though it was treasure. And Eden would always steal it anyway.

Before he could respond, Eden quickly shoved the

rest of the burger into her mouth.

Kai chuckled and slammed his palms onto the table. Reaching across, he clutched her hand. "Come on, I want to take you somewhere."

Kai pulled her across the field and into the cornfield. Letting her hand go, he walked ahead and swam his fingers through the long stalks. She had to jog to keep up with his long legs.

The end of the cornfield turned into a grassy hill and Kai traipsed up, looking back every now and then with a grin on his face. Eden let her hand pinch a leaf on a cornstalk as she stepped onto the hill. Looking ahead, she saw Kai drop to his knees and crawl to the crest.

He waved her over. "Quick, come here, get a load of this."

Déjà vu hit like a sledgehammer. He'd said that before. He'd done that before.

The uniqueness of the area brought a vision barreling to the front of her mind. She ran up the hill, and copying Kai, she dropped to her knees and crawled to the crest.

She'd done that before, too.

When they were ten or eleven and they had no memories from before they were six, they lived there at New Sanctuary. They had no powers, but they knew they were Nephilim and they were told to expect them to return. Eden got the sense that they did everything together and the title "terrible two" echoed through her head.

Eden peered over the hill that sloped down to a small lake. "I remember something," she said, staring at the glistening water. In her memory, Annika stood on the jetty. She was around eighteen and her face was less worn, less hardened by hate. She was smiling and looked effortlessly beautiful. A boy with pure white hair and kohl-lined eyes walked toward her, reaching for her hand to take his. "I see your sister. And... Deacon?"

"Maddox," Kai corrected, sitting up. "Deacon's brother. What happened next?"

Eden stared at the lake as if the memory replayed right in front of her eyes. "They kissed. And we spied on them, the whole time." Eden gave Kai the side-eye. At the time, she felt naughty but also completely thrilled as her and her best friend hid in the grass, watching the exchange. Now, she felt something else.

"And then what happened?" Kai asked, a twinkle in his eyes.

Eden frowned and moved her gaze back to the lake. But nothing came.

"Not with them," Kai teased.

She sat up and faced him. "Huh?"

"This is where we kissed," Kai stated, resting his elbows onto his knees.

Eden sprung to her feet at the same time her heart did the old skip-a-beat thing again. "You're hung up on this kissing memory."

"Maybe I should refresh it for you?" Kai stood.

Eden shook her head, but no words came. If she was honest, she wanted him to. And she hoped he could tell.

Kai's mouth twitched, half-a-smile there and gone in a flash. He turned his palm over. "You said, I wonder what it feels like." He turned his other palm over to mimic scales. "And I said, probably gross." He took a step closer. "Then, you said, let's find out. And then..." Kai moved in, hand hovering but not quite touching her cheek. "I did this—"

He closed the gap, letting his lips bear down on hers. Soft yet quick. At that moment, the memory returned. Two innocent children testing the bounds of their friendship.

In the present, Kai pulled his lips away, his hand still barely touching her face. If Eden was honest again, she wanted more than a peck. Swallowing, she looked into his eyes, hoping he knew that, too.

"Hmm," Kai said, stepping back. "I thought you'd punch my gut like you did before."

Eden shrugged. "I guess we're different now."

Kai raised his brows. "Not really. You're exactly the same, and now that I remember everything, I've never felt more like myself."

He was wrong, Eden thought. She wasn't the same. Weird feelings careened through her and her stupid body reacted in ways she couldn't control. It used to be innocent and light and fun, now it was more than that—heavy and serious. There was a depth to it. She'd changed things between them. "I didn't mean individually. I mean we are different together... Than we were before."

"Are you saying," Kai smirked, "you didn't want to kiss me back then but you want to kiss me now?"

"There you are!" A bellow emerged from the edge of the cornfield.

Kobe and Zahra climbed up the hill, towels draped over their shoulders.

Moving past them, Kobe said, "We're going to the sorry excuse for a lake. You coming?"

Eden

It was autumn. Eden decided there was no way she'd even place a toe in the water. How everyone wanted to go swimming was beyond her.

"Check this," Kobe said, unfurling his wings. They were almost transparent, with shimmers of gold running along the edges of each feather. He leaped into the air and landed on the small cliff hanging over one side of the lake. He let his wings retract and turned around. He threw himself backward into a backflip and slid into the water without a splash.

Eden blinked, a flash of a different place, overtaking her. A lake, different to any other. It was surrounded by rock formations, similar to the cliff Kobe just jumped from. There was a long jetty, reaching out far into the aqua blue water. Eden realized why she liked Lake Louise so much because it reminded her of home. Her real home...

In the distance was a city, houses leading into skyscrapers. The city was divided into seven sections, separated by colors. In her heart, she knew the colors defined who they each were but altogether they were one.

She lifted her hands, small and soft, wrinkled by spending too much time in the water. Across the way, a girl about twelve called out to the cliff-face, "Be careful, you guys. I'll be in so much trouble if you get hurt."

Eden waded around to get a better look. Kai, all six years of age, stood on the cliff's edge. He boomed, "I'm always careful, Annie. I'm a Warrior, just like you." He sat down and dangled his short legs over the rocks. "You should come up here, Edie. The view is so much —"

"Geronimooooo!" Kobe's tiny feet pelted along the stone as he ran past Kai. He curled his legs up into his chest and closed his eyes as he dropped.

Eden closed her eyes as water splashed, ripples rocking her wading body. When she opened her eyes again, everyone had aged.

"Where'd you go?" Kai asked, waiting on the water's edge.

Squeezing her lids shut, Eden tried to grasp onto the vision. She darted them open, declaring, "Lumeria."

Kai gasped. Almost whispering, he said, "Home?"

From behind Eden, two strong arms wrapped around her body. Zahra clutched Eden tight. "Welcome back, Eeds."

Lifting her chin for air, Eden chortled. "I haven't remembered everything yet."

"Doesn't matter," Zahra said, tightening her grasp. "You're still back and you're here to stay."

Kai frowned, moving toward them. His ab muscles rippled as he walked. "What about the rest of them? Don't they deserve to stay too? Don't they deserve the chance at a normal life?"

Zahra let Eden go. She moaned to herself, "Here

we go."

The water rippled as Kobe swam across. He pulled himself out of the lake, eyes locked on Kai. Soaking wet, he inched closer, his face dropping as he saw Kai's serious expression. "Aww, man. I was just getting used to being here with you guys. What's cooking in that brain of yours, Kai? Not another fly through of New York."

Kai whipped his head to Kobe. "What? No. Of course not. We're not twelve anymore."

"Well, then what's your plan?" Zahra said, moving next to Eden.

Heart pounding, Eden watched Kai. She could sense a change in him ever since his full memory returned. It made her wonder what else he'd seen hidden in their past.

Kai flitted his eyes to Eden then to Zahra. "I don't have one."

"Hmm," Zahra crossed her arms and leaned forward, studying his face. "Why don't I believe you?"

A smile sprung across his face. All seriousness had disappeared as he dashed past Zahra and clutched Eden's hand. "I don't know, Z. You tell me." He tugged on Eden's arm and she fell against his side. With his mouth against her ear, he whispered, "We're going to save them all."

Eden's heart soared. And that time it wasn't because of hormonal teenage feelings. It was because she knew, with everything she was, that no matter what it took, they would save their kind. And sure that may sound reckless, but she would rather be that than too scared to move. Maybe, at the end of it all, that's all that would matter. They did something. They took action. They didn't hide in the darkness, hoping that things would change. Yes, they were reckless, but they had heart.

With her arms still crossed, Zahra pouted, looking between Kai and Eden. She opened her mouth to say something, then closed it again and sighed. Licking her lips she tried again, "Because—"

Kai didn't let her finish. He let Eden go, and with two bounding steps, he ran past Kobe and leapt for the lake.

"Because everything you do involves a secret plan," Zahra called after him.

But Eden knew Kai didn't hear her, he was already underwater.

Eden

Dinner came with pasta and meatballs and exuberant smiles. Eden sat at a table with Kai, Zahra, Kobe, and Deacon. It was a friendship that lasted through time.

"I can't believe you went swimming without me," Deacon said, swirling spaghetti with his fork.

Kobe raised his scarred brow. "Seriously? You hate swimming."

"It's still nice to be invited," Deacon mumbled to his food.

Eden placed a gentle hand on his shoulder. "I'll remember you next time."

Deacon tilted his head and showed her a sideways half-smile. "I know you will, Eeds. You're the nice one of this bunch."

"Hey!" Zahra protested.

Eden grinned, her attention turning to her food. She stabbed a meatball, letting her mind drift back to her most recent memory. To Lumeria.

The city was sectioned by the Archangel

descendants. Seven of them. Mentally, she listed through them:

Azrael, the Transporters.

Michael, the Warriors.

Jophiel, the Elementals.

Chamuel, the Shields.

Raphael, the Healers.

Ariel, the Shifters.

Who was the seventh? Did she remember incorrectly? Dropping her fork, she blurted, "Are there six or seven Archangels?"

Amused, but not surprised by her outburst, Zahra replied, "Technically there are eight."

"Yeah," Deacon muttered. "But we don't count Lucifer's offspring. Traitorous bastards."

"Lucifer," Eden repeated. They must have been the other section at Lumeria, but that knowledge didn't feel quite right. Like there was something else still missing.

Kobe rolled his eyes. "Bunch of wimps and cowards, they are. No one's seen them in the extraction chamber or cages. In fact, no one's seen a single one since the ambush twelve years ago."

"Wow," Eden mused, returning to her food. But then—"Wait. You said there are eight Archangels?"

Kai cleared his throat and calmly placed his fork onto the table. His eyes darted to Eden, then back to his food. "Gabriel," he said, picking up his fork again. Quickly, he added, "But he doesn't have descendants."

Eden nodded. "Okay." A little bit satisfied but mostly overwhelmed, she was happy to end the conversation. Talking with them became tiring at times like she was always a few steps behind. It was like trying to solve an equation without the right formula.

Across the hall, Eden noticed Jia. She was sitting with a Healer Angel and every few seconds she'd glance over her shoulder at Eden. There was an unspoken bond between them. Of family, but also that they were at similar stages of returning.

On Jia's next peek, Eden quickly waved her over. Jia swiped her plate and jumped up, almost knocking her seat over, she stormed across the room and slid into the seat next to Zahra. Beaming with enthusiasm, she practically shouted, "Hi, Eden."

Kobe coughed, almost choking on his food. He peered around Zahra to see who'd joined them. When his eyes found Jia, he returned her beaming expression.

"Um, guys," Eden said as calmly as possible. "You know Jia, right? She's my cousin."

"Hi, Jia," Kai said immediately. Deacon waved his fork as a greeting. And the twins both smiled politely.

"It's okay if you don't remember me," Jia said, followed by a nervous laugh. "I've been locked up for twelve years."

Silence.

It was understandable to Eden, that words felt meaningless. Four of them had experienced a portion of what she had. Although, the twins only once a long time ago. And Eden couldn't really remember anything about her times there except Kai behind glass. Kai seemed the most sympathetic to Jia's statement, Eden could see it in his eyes that he was trying to imagine a whole life in that place.

"It sucks." Kai winced as though he wished better words were coming out.

"You know," Deacon said, not looking up. "I bet you're loving this food."

Jia's eyes lit up. She smiled at Deacon, even though he couldn't see it. "Oh, am I ever! I can't get enough. I literally sneak in here when everyone is sleeping and scarf on cookie dough. Is that not the best thing ever?" She looked around the table, her face dropping. "Oh no. I shouldn't have said that. Will you tell on me?"

Zahra chuckled. "Your secret is safe with me."

"But how about next time, you invite me?" said Kai, a cheeky grin on his face.

"Of course," Eden teased, nudging him with her elbow. "You'd be in on anything to do with food."

"Ha!" Deacon burst, finally lifting his gaze to Jia. He pointed his fork in her direction. "Just a tip, don't trust Kai around food. It gets nasty."

As Deacon's eyes landed on Jia, she visibly sucked in her breath. Trying to contain a smile, she asked, "Oh, really?"

"Yeah, watch this." Deacon reached across Eden and stabbed his fork into one of Kai's meatballs.

Kai quickly pierced his own fork through, and as Deacon tried to slide it off the plate, Kai jerked it back again.

The meatball split in two.

Sauce splattered across the table.

A droplet landed on Zahra's forehead.

In shock, Zahra's mouth fell open. She slowly grabbed a napkin and wiped herself clean. Beside her, Kobe stifled a laugh. She whipped her head. "Is that funny, brother?"

"Hilarious," he stated, mouth full of pasta.

"Oh yeah? What about this?" Zahra picked up a strand of spaghetti between her fingers and placed it carefully on top of her brother's head.

As the strand slid over his ear, Kobe dropped his fork and slammed his hand into his dinner. He grabbed a handful of sauce and meat and spaghetti and threw it. Except, it didn't hit Zahra. It flew right past her and landed on Jia. Globs of meatball dripped down her neck, small clusters of sauce rolling onto her white top.

Jia gasped, staring at the mess. She pressed her middle finger into her thumb and flicked half a meatball from her chest across the table. It went hurtling in Deacon's direction, and without batting an eye, he backhanded the incoming chow away.

It hit Eden, catching in her hair. She pried the offending piece of food out and gleefully swiveled to face Kai. But before she could throw it, he'd taken her fork swirled with pasta, and flung it back to Deacon.

Soon the whole table was a riot. Food flying in all directions. Laughter and squeals of delight echoed around the hall. People looked over, some with disdain, some with jealousy, but most with amusement.

It all ended abruptly when the door opened and Annika stepped through.

Her cold stare landed on Kai's table and noticing the mess, she rolled her eyes. Eden froze, watching Annika's movements with bated breath. She didn't know her too well, but she knew that type of behavior definitely wouldn't be approved. But much to Eden's surprise, instead of getting angry, Annika calmly walked to the serving tray and dished herself up a meal. She wandered to a table without another glance in their direction and proceeded to eat in silence.

A collective sigh echoed around the table.

"Okay, guys," Kai said, picking up his fork. He dragged an overhanging strand of pasta back onto his plate. "We should do what we are meant to with food now. You know, eat it?"

"I blame Jia," Deacon teased, before slurping what remained of his dinner.

Eden

The sun was setting. Its last rays speckled through the tops of the trees, casting a golden hue over the evergreen pine nettles. Layers of light pink and orange reached into darkening blue.

Eden inhaled, long and loud. "I haven't seen a proper sunset in forever."

Smooth fingers slid through hers and clasped tight. Kai said, "We used to watch them here all the time, do you remember?"

Eden nodded; she remembered a lot of small moments. She searched the field and pointed to a spot just before the closest mountain. A spray of light beamed down like a torch. "We'd sit there because that's where the last ray of light would shine through the trees."

Smiling, Kai tugged on her hand, leading her to the spot. They sat on the cooling grass and Kai gazed at Eden, eyes crinkling. He reached into his jacket inside pocket and retrieved two wrapped candies.

"What ya got there?" Eden asked, knowing exactly

what it was.

"Caramel," he replied, placing it in front of her. "I took a note out of Jia's book and stole them from the kitchen."

"Thank you."

Without touching the candy, Eden lifted it off the ground and untwisted the wrapper with her mind. She swiped the candy and shoved it into her mouth. The wrapper hung in the air for a moment, while she savored the first taste, and then she scrunched the plastic and telekinetically put it in her pocket.

Impressed, Kai's bottom lip rolled out. "Wow, you've come a long way in just a day."

"Mm," Eden mumbled around the caramel chew. "I still can't do the portal thing though."

He reached his hand to her cheek, and the touch made her heart flip. As he tilted his head, Eden thought for sure he was going to kiss her again. A slight tug on her hair and he pulled away, holding up pinched fingers that held a broken strand of pasta.

Flicking it away, he said, "You used to be the best at it."

"I did?"

As if they were in a crowded room, Kai leaned over, so close she could feel his breath on her cheek, and whispered, "Wyatt's portals are babies compared to yours."

That's all it took. A few words of encouragement. Determined, she placed her hands together and looked out at the forest edge a few meters away. Eden separated her hands and stared at the space between them, willing and urging something to appear. A tiny flicker of purple sparked and then disappeared.

"That's it," Kai urged, sitting up on his knees. "You can do this, Edie."

Eden made herself comfortable on her knees and sat up straight. She brought her hands together, took a quick breath, then slowly pulled them apart. Another purple spark appeared. She widened her hands, and the spark popped, opening into a small circle. Pine nettles became close enough to touch. She let the portal hover in the air in front of her and reached her hand through the circle.

Pulling out a twig, Eden beamed. "That was easy."

She twisted her wrist and closed the portal. The smallest twinkle of purple lingered, and she wiggled her fingers to remove the remnant.

"I told you," Kai said.

Eden lunged forward and threw her arms around his neck. He hugged her back, tightly. Letting go, she gasped, "I've gotta show Wyatt."

She jumped to her feet and opened a portal to the food hall. Through the small circle, she saw Wyatt sitting at a table near the server, chatting with Annika. Eden closed the portal and opened a new one, closer.

This time the portal hovered at the end of the table Wyatt was at. He looked up, surprised. Eden expanded her arms, stretching the portal big enough to walk through. Kai stepped through after her, bobbing his head to fit.

Eden closed the portal and proud of her effort, she spun to face Wyatt, smiling at him with excited anticipation. She didn't even feel out of breath, not like Jia had. "What do you think?"

"I..." he glanced around her with wide eyes, "I think..."

"You forgot to remove the remnant," Annika stated in a monotone.

Kai huffed and retorted, "Give her credit where it's due."

Untying his tongue, Wyatt said, "You're a fast learner, Eeds."

Kai leaned over to Wyatt, and glancing at Eden, he whispered. Wyatt eyed Eden, a wry smile growing. He nodded at Kai and stood. "Come with me."

The two of them scurried off and Eden was left with Annika, standing in awkward silence. Annika cleared her throat. Eden gave a quick smile and slumped into the chair where Wyatt was.

"I know he's planning something," Annika said, leaning back deep into her chair.

"What?" Eden said, pretending to be vague while replaying Kai's words in her mind. *"We're going to save everyone."*

Annika spread her fingers through her hair and sighed. "I know you're thinking about leaving and doing something stupid."

"At least we want to do something," Eden muttered, turning away, hoping to see Kai.

Annika touched Eden's arm, and as Eden turned back, she saw a softer expression on Annika's face. "Listen, I get it. He's brave. He's oh, so just and righteous. But, he's stupid. Always running into things, thinking he can solve all the problems with his presence alone. It doesn't work like that."

"But isn't—" Eden started.

Throwing her arms in the air, Annika said, "And now his little sister is captured and—"

"Well, isn't it a good thing for us to leave?" Eden interrupted; frustration evident by the wrinkles on her forehead. "So we can find her?"

Annika rolled her eyes and sat back in the chair again. "What? For him to be caught again? You know how dangerous that is, right?"

It didn't make sense to Eden, why no one at New Sanctuary was willing to fight. Why would it be so dangerous to leave? Sure they might lose their powers and memories, but wasn't it worth it, to make sure their people had a chance at normal lives?

"I know it's a sacrifice," Eden reasoned, "But the memories and powers come back, eventually. In Kai's case, a few days."

"Ugh," Annika moaned. She pushed her chair back, scraping the legs along the floor. "That's stupid and naïve, even for you."

The words stung.

Annika stood over Eden, her blue eyes fierce and

commanding. "Wait until your full memory returns, then we can talk about it again."

Eden watched Annika storm off, leaving her feeling less than herself. What was she missing? What was so bad about trying to help their fellow Nephilim? Sighing, she slumped forward, tapping the table leg with her foot.

"Edie?" A sweet voice cooed.

Kai jogged across the hall with a grin, wagging something in his hands. Reaching her, his smile faded, "What's wrong..." His eyes darted to Annika's empty chair. "Did she say something?"

Standing up, Eden put on her best smile. "It doesn't matter, what were you doing?"

"Oh, right." Kai lifted his hand and wiggled the keys. "I want to show you something."

Kai

Behind the living barn was a small garage. Kai lifted the roller door and stepped inside. He gave Eden a quick smile as he clutched a dusty white sheet and pulled it back, revealing Wyatt's old jeep.

Eden stared at it; eyes wide. She glanced up to Kai, the biggest grin on her face. "Are we leaving New Sanctuary?"

The look on her face made him happy. It was exactly the reaction he was after. "Nah... not yet. I want to show you something. Hop in."

They jumped into the door-less car and he shoved the key into the ignition. Kai ticked it over and swung his head in her direction. "Seatbelt."

As soon as the belt clicked into the buckle, Kai floored the accelerator, tearing out of the garage. Eden flung her hands to the dashboard as he tore down a gravel road and into the forest. Wind whipped against his face as he weaved around corners, changing gears like a pro. Loving every second.

"I think I'm gonna be sick," Eden said, leaning forward.

Kai swore under his breath and relaxed his foot off the gas. "I'll slow down." He switched his gaze between the road in front of him to Eden, and when he saw her rest back against the seat, he let his eyes drift back to the road. "I thought you would have enjoyed this. It's a little like flying."

"Mm-hmm," Eden said, rolling her head to him. "Just like eating vanilla is a little like caramel... it's not."

"Point taken," Kai chuckled, taking a left turn.

The road steepened, and in a little while, the trees made way for sky. Kai parked the car as close to the cliff edge as possible. He watched Eden as she shuffled to the edge of her seat, staring into the distance.

"It's..." The only thing she could say.

That was the next reaction he was after. Kai nodded to himself, satisfied, as his best friend gawked at the scene in front of them.

They were at a lookout, not quite halfway up the mountain, but still high enough to see at least fifty miles. From there, they could see the valley weave between the ebbs and flows of smaller hills. Scattered lights of nearby towns glistened below as stars twinkled above.

Eden clutched the side of the jeep and Kai could tell she wanted to be out there, closer, amongst it all. He tapped the wheel twice. "Come on."

The air was cool, and the sun was gone. Kai leaned against the hood of the car and watched Eden teeter to the edge. She stopped, toes bending over the rocky cliff. The thought of her falling, without her wings, sent his mind to the pit of Hell and back. Kai pushed himself off the car. "Be careful."

Smirking, she glanced back at him. "If I fell, you'd save me, right?"

Kai swallowed, not enjoying the teasing look on her face. "Come on, Eden, it's safer back here."

"Are you scared, Warrior boy?" She held her arms wide and peered down below.

He didn't like it.

It was no different to how they were with each other before they got separated. He teased her, she mocked him. It was a mutual friendship of cheek and comfort. But she was right, they were different together than they were before. The way he felt about her had deepened. He'd changed things between them.

"What would you do, if I just..." Eden bent her knees, threatening to jump.

Not even a second passed, and Kai had lunged for her, wrapping his arms around her torso. He kept his feet on the ground, steady, while his wings arched out behind him, readying for flight. His chest pressed against her back, lungs increasing their intake.

Eden tilted her head to him, her demeanor subdued. She was no longer smiling. Her voice hitched as she said, "I'd never actually do it."

He wanted to turn her around and kiss her, clutch her shoulders tight and pull her in close to him. He wanted to feel her soft lips and taste her tongue. With the starry sky above them and the damp forest floor at their feet, holding her like that, it wasn't enough.

But it had to be enough. He needed to wait for her full memory to return. Betraying his own heart, he took a few steps back and let her go.

Returning to the view, Eden crossed her arms and rubbed. There was a slight shiver dancing across her shoulders.

"Are you cold?" Kai asked, taking off his jacket.

"No." Eden shook her head. Through chattering teeth, she said, "I'm fine."

"You're not fine," he scolded and placed it over her back. "You're freezing."

Eden rolled her shoulders, letting the jacket drop to the ground. Gravel compressed beneath her heels as she spun around. "I said I'm fine."

Frowning, Kai picked up his jacket. He dusted it off, wondering if he said something wrong. "Listen, I'm sorry if I—"

"Shut up," Eden scolded. She scuffed her feet along the ground as she walked to the car, and sat in the passenger seat, legs still outside.

"What?" Kai followed her with caution.

Sighing, she looked up, tears lining her face. "No one gets to see this." She threw her hand in the direction of the twinkling lights in distant streets below. "Not at night. Not anymore. Because of me."

Kai burst with sadness as he watched Eden crumble before his eyes. Her shoulders quaked as she sobbed into her hands. He rushed to her, and with one hand cupping the roof of the car, his other peeled her hands off her face. She dropped her hands but refused to look at him.

"Edie, stop it," he begged. Knowing that wasn't going to be good enough. "You can't hold that guilt. It's not your fault, none of this nonsense is your fault." Still clutching the roof, he let his free hand pinch her chin, gently, so as not to hurt her. He lifted her face to his and her reddened eyes met his. "You know whose fault it is, don't you? Corrupt humans. Hunters. They're the ones who started this, they're the ones who keep everyone from the night. Not us. Don't you dare carry that."

Nodding, Eden pulled down the sleeves of her hoodie and wiped her face.

Kai knew she only agreed to appease him. Even he didn't believe his own words. It was their fault. His fault. New York was her idea, but he was more than happy to follow her lead, every time he'd follow her lead. She didn't know yet, that she was the one with all the ideas, and that he was the one to tag along with her to the ends of the earth.

It wasn't just New York. It was her, when they were five, still at Lumeria, opening portals across every continent, peeking into lands to spy on the humans. Kai often wondered if that's what brought the Hunters to them. It was her, when the Hunters attacked, who tried to distract them away from Kai, but ended up leading them to all her cousins. It was her at New Sanctuary, right after their powers returned and before New York, who overheard Alistair talking about how certain people traded Nephilim for money. She tried to sneak him, Deacon, and the twins, into the home of a Hunter. But New York—that was the one Annika hated him for the most.

Eden didn't know, and that was okay for now. He'd taken the blame for all of it. He let Annika beat the shit out of him every time they fought, he let all the remaining Nephilim stare at him with disdain, he'd let them all think Eden was his poor sidekick, being dragged into things because of his outlandish plans. He'd do it again for the next six-year cycle and the one after that, and any more that followed, if that's what it took.

Kai held out his jacket. Eden rolled her eyes, swiped it from him, and wrapped the warm leather around her. They shared a look, gray eyes to aqua, a promise. Unspoken yet acknowledged—they were going to fix it, together.

On the drive back, Eden said, "You can go faster, now, if you want. I think I'll be okay."

"Are you sure?" Kai asked, re-grasping the steering wheel in preparation.

A wry smile crept across her face. "Remember that time we escaped Nancy's and you didn't know how to drive a self-piloted car?"

"Hey!" Kai chuckled, pleased to see her back to normal. "I got it to work. At least I wasn't delirious."

She chortled. And then her eyes drifted forward, a strange look casting over her. Skin turning pale, she clutched at his hand that rested on the shift.

"Malakai!" she commanded. "Stop the car."

25

Eden

Eden didn't know why she hadn't realized it before. When their car had run out of electricity and they had to walk to the border, they saw a boy. She told Kai not to intervene, why did she do that? That boy was a descendant of Raphael, his name was Luca. He was a Healer Angel, taken and locked up, used for his grace.

She sat up straight. Another face she knew but failed to recognize at the most important time. Back at Nancy's, before they escaped, she saw someone. A girl. She had white hair and hopeful blue eyes...

A flutter circled Eden's stomach.

"Stop the car," she ordered him again.

He slammed on the brakes, eyes wide open, searching the forest for danger. "What is it?"

"I know where Harper is."

Kai

Kai wanted to wait until everyone was asleep, to avoid any inquiries from Annika. Her mat was in the middle of the room, covered with a velvet blanket. It was blue. Like everything she owned. All to honor a father they'd never met.

He'd spent most of his time gazing at the ceiling, trying not to cry. He'd been in the same house as his sister and didn't even know it. Her innocent face flew in circles through his mind. He dabbed at a tear that was forming in his eye and rolled over.

Eden faced him, asleep, eyes fluttering in a dream. Kai marveled that she was just as beautiful asleep as she was awake. Once he laid his eyes on her in that state, it was hard to tear himself away.

They'd always been best friends. He'd always loved her. But this time it was different. He loved her more than a friend should. There was no turning back now.

Her delicate hand hung out the side of her mat and he tilted his head to check the time on her watch. It was well past one o'clock in the morning. Certain that his movements wouldn't wake anyone else, he gently shook Eden's shoulders.

As her eyes blinked open, he whispered, "It's time."

Giving her a moment to wake, Kai crept around her mat and knelt above Deacon. He hovered over his head, wondering how to ask him such a big favor. Deacon twitched and rolled to his back, peeling one eye open. He shut it again and moaned, "What's my part in your plan?"

That's what Kai always liked about Deacon. He was abrasive and melancholy most of the time, but he was also fiercely loyal and ready to help any way he was needed. "That's my man," Kai whispered. He pointed to the twins beside them. "Wake them up and meet me outside."

Kai craned his neck to look at the sky. "I don't think I said thank you."

"What for?" Eden asked, rubbing her arms.

They stood in the middle of the field, waiting for the others. A cool breeze rolled through the valley. Kai noticed the clear night, speckled with twinkling stars. The perfect conditions for flying.

"For remembering my sister," Kai said, his gaze falling to Eden.

The blue dye had almost faded from her hair, and as the moonlight hit her white streak, it practically glowed. She shrugged with a shiver. "If I had any control over my memories, I would have remembered everything six years ago. Or at least recognized her when I saw her."

Kai stepped closer to block the chilly breeze from hitting her. "I hope she's still there."

Eden gave him a look as if she'd noticed he'd moved purposefully to stop her from being so cold. The ends of her mouth twitched into a barely noticeable smile. Kai felt his heart burn. There was nothing he wouldn't do to protect her and he hoped she was starting to realize that.

She slid her fingertips over the back of his hand and threaded them through. Her eyes deepened as she moved closer. With a whisper, she said, "Kai?"

The way she spoke his name sent his pulse into overdrive. Blood coursed through his veins. He swept his fingers through the side of her hair, watching the moonlight bounce off her streak. It didn't hold his gaze for long, before his eyes cast on her lips, slightly open, full and waiting. The space between them decreased. And right when he was ready to lose himself in her kiss, footsteps came thumping.

"What's going—oh, sorry are we interrupting?" Zahra stopped in her tracks, looking between Eden and Kai.

Even in the dark, Kai could see the blood that flushed Eden's cheeks. He cleared his throat and turned to his friends. "No, I want you guys here. Eden has a... I have a mission for us."

Kobe ran his hand over his buzz cut and yawned. "Does it involve flying through a city?"

"No," Kai spat, offended. Then, with a softer voice, he said, "We're going to New Jersey. Eden remembered where Harper is... was... could be."

"Let's go, then," Kobe said, his tone matching Kai's.

Zahra pulled her curly hair back off her face and tugged a hair tie from her wrist to tie it up. She slid another one off and passed it to Eden. "Tip for flying, always bring a hair tie."

"I, uh, I can't fly yet." Eden slowly took the tie from Zahra and began pulling her hair back.

Kai watched as parts of her fringe fell out immediately. Endeared, he said, "We can do what we did last time."

Eden blushed again.

"Listen," Kai said, silently scolding himself for

being distracted. He faced Deacon and the twins. "I'm not gonna lie, it's a dangerous mission. We're going to a halfway house. It belongs to a woman named Nancy." He turned to Eden. "You know how I had to get out of there? My soul remembered something my mind couldn't. I'd been there before last week. Nancy held me there. I was weakened by that clasp she had and she handed me over for extraction."

"Alistair told me about her," Zahra said. "She's a middle-man... middle-woman. She trades both ways. She's how we get some of us back. Once a year, Alistair gathers enough money to buy a Nephilim back. Eden, you, Kai, most recently Jia, and I guess, Kai again."

"Wait, wait, wait. Back up." Deacon looked down his nose. "A halfway house? Haven't we tried that before?"

"We have?" Eden asked.

Dammit, Kai didn't want to bring up things she hadn't remembered yet. It was just a silly mission. Eden eavesdropped on Alistair for info and found a halfway house address. They were going to break in and torture them to give up the location of where they kept the Nephilim but got caught before they'd gone too far.

"Yeah," Kai muttered, trying to brush it off. "That doesn't count, we didn't get very far."

"We were lucky," Deacon huffed.

"Ha!" Kobe crowed. "I don't think Wyatt kicking our asses was lucky."

"We got lucky," Deacon repeated with a scowl. He sniffed and averted his gaze.

Kai felt his blood rise. Shifting between feet, he clenched his fists. "Okay, well, anyway. This Hunter's got Harper. So we're doing this, right now. Knowing the risks, are you in?"

Without hesitation, Zahra and Kobe said yes.

Deacon kept his eyes to the barn and grimaced.

Kai thought for sure, he would decide to sit this one out. But, as always, Deacon was full of surprises. He rolled his shoulders and his wings spanned out. As he lifted off the ground, he said, "What are you losers waiting for?"

Eden

Blue and opalescent wings spanned six meters from one tip to the other. They moved strong, up and down, as they soared in the open air. Eden loved Kai's wings, and she knew she always had. She felt his heart beat against her ribs as he held her in his arms, hundreds of feet off the ground.

Above them, Deacon flew. His rose gold wings emitted a kind of shimmer that expanded like an umbrella overhead. She never noticed that before. He had a stern expression as he looked forward, eyes unfaltering on their course. The blood on his lip from when she first met him, again, was now barely even a scratch.

"What's his deal?" Eden asked.

Kai glanced up. "Deacon?"

"Yeah. I mean..." Eden winced, trying to word it properly. "He's nice. But he seems to carry something heavy with him."

Nodding, Kai said, "His brother, Maddox... He

died."

"Oh." Eden's heart burst open. She wanted to reach up and hug Deacon and his broken heart that was forever changed by grief. "I didn't know."

"No, you wouldn't have remembered it, either. It was after we were taken when we were twelve. He left New Sanctuary to search for us, but he got caught for the first time."

She turned her attention back to Kai. "How did he die?"

Grimacing, Kai said, "You don't remember, do you?"

"You just said I wouldn't remember." Eden was confused.

"No, I mean—" Kai paused to lick his lips. "What happens to teenagers or adults when their grace is extracted?"

"They forget who they are and lose their powers for a few years?" Eden answered the question but the way his face dropped, she knew she was wrong.

Kai inhaled shakily before replying, "There isn't really a specific age limit, Annika thinks it's puberty, but if a pure is extracted over the age of fourteen to sixteen, there's a high chance it will kill them. And for adults, if they're pures or not, it's a definite."

Gasping, Eden looked away. Harper. She was pure and fourteen. No wonder Annika was so mad.

"I guess we were lucky to have been extracted so young," Zahra said, flying closer. "Especially you, Kai, no one's ever been extracted three times and survived."

Eden didn't think it was lucky though. None of it was luck. It was sacrificial genocide.

"Did you hear the whole conversation?" Kai asked Zahra, shifting a worried eye up to Deacon.

"Don't worry." Zahra's voice was comforting. "He's too transfixed on projecting his shield around us. He's hopeless at multi-tasking."

Below them, drones buzzed about their routes. At that moment, Eden realized how much Deacon cared about them. He'd never say it but he didn't have to, his actions spoke volumes. As a pure, he risked his own life to leave New Sanctuary and protect them.

Once they hit New Jersey, their elevation dropped. Deacon stayed close to Kai and followed his directions to Nancy's. When they reached the right street, they all descended.

Deacon kept them covered as they stood across the road and one house down, hovering behind a tree. Around them, drapes were drawn and doors locked. Quiet. Eden guessed in that time zone, it would be around three-thirty in the morning.

"I should have done this before when we first got here," Eden said, lifting her wrist and flicking the projection up. There were no red dots in the house. "She's not there."

"Well, she could be." Kai leaned over her, getting a peek for himself.

Eden tapped the blueprint of the house. "No, she's not. Hunters show up red, remember?"

"I know. But maybe she isn't a Hunter."

Eden thought back to when they met Nancy and shook her head. "I saw her neck; it was like those men at my apartment."

"She didn't have black eyes."

"Well," Eden spluttered, getting frustrated. "Maybe she's something else."

Kai smirked and said, "Something that doesn't show up on your watch?"

Silence.

Ugh, he was right. A few days ago they didn't know what a Hunter was, God knows what else there is out there. She expanded the area of blueprint, widening the vision to the whole street, just in case.

Kai's smile faded as his hand found her shoulder. "Let's just take it as though she's home. To be safe."

Eden noticed the blue dots where they stood across the road. "Kai, look," she said pointing. The other four were a darker shade of blue than Eden's, although hers had brightened some. "I think the colors represent memory."

Kai smiled softly. He let his hand slide down between her shoulder blades, right where wings would grow. "The color shows your power."

Eden slumped her shoulders. "I don't think Harper's here—"

"Look," he interrupted, pointing to the house's blueprint. Another blue dot, even fainter than Eden's, paced in a bedroom up the top floor. "That's her. That's Harper."

"How can you be sure?" Eden asked, squinting at the projector. The light was so dull, she had missed it before.

"Call it an instinct." Kai smiled knowingly and shrugged. He kicked his heels up and began running across the street. Swiveling around, he ran backward and mouthed, "Quick!"

Deacon and the twins hurried to follow him. Adopting Kai's excitement, Eden grinned and ran, catching up to them on the edge of the lawn.

On the second floor, in the room on the right, the drapes were held open. A young girl with platinum hair gaped at them through the glass. Her eyes lifted into first a smile and then a grin. She quickly and quietly opened the window.

"I'll keep the shield up," Deacon said, flying above the house. He settled on the roof and kept his wings opened wide. A pink shimmer cloaked the whole house.

"Kobe, Zahra!" Kai pointed to the front door. "You're on watch."

The twins shifted. Kobe into an owl and Zahra into a small cat. Kobe flew to a nearby tree and Zahra ran to the porch, pacing along a banister.

"Are you ready?" Kai asked Eden. And before she had a chance to answer, he wrapped his arms around her and rose to the open window.

Inside, the room was sparse, occupied only by a mattress on the floor and a girl cowering in the corner. As soon as Kai lowered Eden down, the girl ran for him.

"I knew you'd come back for me," she whispered, flinging her arms around his neck.

Welcoming the embrace, Kai muttered into her hair, "I'm so sorry. I never should have brought you into all of this."

"It's okay. It was my choice to follow you." Harper stepped back. "And then I saw her capture you and I... I couldn't leave you. I wanted to go back for help but I know Annie would never risk more lives. So, I made the choice to save you. But I was too late. I hid in those bushes down the street and saw them take you. I was so angry." Harper bunched her fists into little balls by her sides. She started pacing the room. "I wanted her to pay. I planned to sneak in here and hurt her, make her tell me where the hideout was so I could do something... anything." She stopped walking and stared at the peeling wallpaper. Turning around, she lifted her wrist, encircled with a bronze clasp. "But she captured me instead. They are coming for me tomorrow."

Harper's tears made Eden lurch forward. She clutched her elbow. "They're not coming for you, not ever. I promise."

Nodding, Harper sniffed and wiped her wet cheeks. She looked at Kai, her eyes dancing over his brown hair. "How do you remember me?"

"I'd never forget you," Kai said, joining them. He tucked Harper's hair behind her ear and gave Eden a quick glare.

Eden knew what the look meant. It meant not to tell Harper the truth—that they both had forgotten who she was.

"Is Nancy here?" Eden asked, moving to the door.

Harper's face lifted. "Yeah, she's probably downstairs getting high. I can't leave the house or this stupid clasp will siren, trust me I've tried. But... well... follow me."

She tiptoed to the door, opened it slightly, then put an ear to the hallway. Distant sounds of the television echoed from downstairs. Satisfied, she opened the door fully and stepped into the hallway. She crept across the mezzanine, casting an eye down to the living room archway as she went. At the end of the hall, she stopped at a door and turned the handle. As the door clicked open, she turned around and pointed to Kai and Eden, then lifted a finger to her mouth.

Eden gave an amused frown, glancing at Kai to see if he found it odd, too. He didn't return her glance though, instead nodding once to Harper in agreement. Following his lead, Eden ran her fingers along her lips to zip them shut. Harper took a quick breath, then entered the room.

Kai followed her and as soon as he was in the room, he exclaimed, "Oh my God!"

Curious, Eden walked in. Kai was standing in the middle of the room, his arms around someone, and someone's arms were around him. Her heart leapt; she'd recognize those strong hands anywhere.

"Dad?" she asked.

28

Eden

Nothing could have prepared Eden for the sight of her parents. As Kai stepped away, she saw her dad, and behind him, her mom. They were wearing the same bronze bracelets as Harper, except they also had chains that connected the bracelets to a bar on the wall. They looked tired and malnourished.

Eden felt a storm of relief and rage swirl inside her.

When Lacey spotted Eden, her shoulder's dropped. "What are you doing?" she hissed in a whisper. "You can't be here."

"Yes, you both need to leave." Alistair tried to push Kai back, but even he couldn't make the Warrior Angel budge. Frustrated, he swung his arm to the window. "Take Harper and go."

"No." Eden shook her head. How dare they push her away. After everything she'd been through the last few days. "I thought I'd lost you both. Now, I've found you, I'm not going to leave you like this!"

Lacey's knees buckled. "Oh, my stubborn child."

Eden ran to her, slowing Lacey's fall to the ground. She looked at the bronze clasp, her eyes followed the chain all the way to the bolt on the wall. Being this close, Eden's powers would be useless against it.

"Quick, Malakai, break this." Harper held out her hand. Kai tried to break the clasp apart but the dampener inside it spilled through, rendering his strength useless.

Eden ran to the door, away from anyone with a clasp. With her mind, she imagined Harper's clasp weakening from the inside out. The clasp snapped under the pressure and Eden turned to her parents, doing the same for them. Harper rushed to Alistair, using her renewed strength to break the chains, and Kai helped Lacey.

Joy erupted as Eden crashed into her father's arms. She held him tight, promising herself to never run away and leave him to fight alone again, no matter what he told her to do. A gentle hand smoothed around her shoulder as Lacey joined them. Cradled in her parents' arms, tears of what-ifs and repressed denial fell in waves down Eden's face. They were alive. Nothing else mattered in that moment.

The door slammed shut. Eden broke away from the embrace, craning her neck to see who caused it. Nancy Withers scowled at her intruders. Below her chin, black veins pulsated along her neck like a spider's web.

"You children will die. You hear me?" she crowed. "It's your fault this is happening to me."

Wondering what on earth she meant, Eden eyed Nancy carefully. Fingers twitched manically at her sides, the nail of her middle finger flicking against the bud of her thumb. She was wincing as though in pain but her shoulders were rolled back like she had the strength of an ox. She lifted a small radio to her mouth. "Widow to Base. I have three Nephilim in my possession, requesting immediate collection. Ov—"

Eden swiftly raised her hand and flung the radio across the room. She turned to Nancy, stepping closer. "What's your move? I know you're strong. Somehow. But you know you're no match for us, right?"

"You'll pay for what you've done to us," Kai scowled, moving next to Eden.

"What I've done to you?" A cackle bounced off the walls. Nancy pointed wildly at her neck and pulled at her collar, baring her shoulder. The black veins ran across her clavicle and pooled at the front of her shoulder. "What about what you've done to me?"

Eden frowned. She had no idea what Nancy was talking about.

"Give it a rest, sad sack," Harper said with a teenage attitude. "You're the one who chose to inject yourself with grace. It's not our fault how humans' bodies react to it."

"What?" Kai said, whipping his head to Harper. "Is that why we are being extracted? For what? Drugs? A quick high?"

"Oh, it's not quick," Nancy's tone switched from whiny to arrogant. "It's forever. The more we get the stronger we are. The smarter we are. The better we are."

Eden thought about the Hunters who attacked her home and tried to kill her. Their black eyes deeper than Nancy's pale greens and their black blood thick like goo. "You won't be better. But I think you know that."

"Shut up," Nancy snapped.

The more Eden thought about it, the more despondent she felt. The whole prospect made her heart sink. The Nephilim were nothing but a commodity, used for a select few humans' gain. Their lives didn't matter. Their deaths didn't matter, as long as the Hunters got what they needed.

"Is this all we're good for?" she wondered out loud. "Is this all we're worth?"

"Eden!" Alistair scolded. "Now's not the time. She's stalling you. We have to go."

A wide grin grew across Nancy's face. She checked her watch. "I just need two more minutes."

She danced her eyes over the other five in the room, her gaze locking onto Harper. A cry for war lingered in the air as she lunged forward, pushing Harper to the floor. Kai pulled her off with one hand and flung her across the room. Nancy hit the window frame, cracking the pane a little.

Her threatening smile dropped as she regained her composure. Blood started seeping down the side of her face. After wiping it she checked her hand, almost surprised to see the crimson shade laced with thin black streaks. She cranked her neck to the side once, then let out another cry. Forward, she galloped toward Kai, a violent intent in her eyes.

Before she reached him… long before she got even close, Eden swung her arm forward. Her powers were easy to control, a simple wish was enough to turn her thoughts into telekinetic energy. Nancy hung in the air, mid-step, frozen by Eden's will.

Eden considered her next move. Nancy was no match for her, even in her drugged-up state. Eden could crush her from the inside out if she wanted, all with a simple thought.

"Eden," Lacey warned. "If we're going to leave, we need to leave now."

"Give her what she deserves," Harper jeered. She bounced from foot to foot, clenched fists hanging by her sides. There was no doubting she was a daughter of the Angel of War.

Eden looked at Nancy as she hovered in the middle of the room, limbs limp and mouth agape. "Have mercy," Nancy begged. "I'm just a broker."

If Harper and Kai were the children of Michael, Angel of War, then shouldn't she as the daughter of Azrael, Angel of Death, want to end Nancy for good?

But the look of sincere terror on Nancy's face sent flutters through Eden's heart. No. She didn't want to kill her. Just like she didn't want to kill the Hunters in the conservatory.

The sound of the front door bursting open interrupted Eden's decision. A flurry of gentle footsteps bounded up the stairs and a tabby cat entered the room. Zahra shifted and puffed. "We have company."

Eden dropped Nancy where she was and Kai sped to contain her in his hold. He grabbed the chains that held Lacey and Alistair and tied Nancy up. The decision was made for her. Nancy lived.

"Guys?" Kobe's voice rattled on the landing.

"In here!" Eden called, running to the door.

Spotting her, Kobe ran. Deacon was closing behind him. And behind them both, a pack of four Hunters.

The two Nephilim slid into the room and Zahra slammed the door shut, making sure to lock it. Spinning around, she hastened, "Are we going to fight?"

Harper pushed herself to the door. With flared nostrils, she said, "We've got this."

"No." Kai tumbled over himself to get to her. "You don't have this. We can't risk it; we have to get out of here. Open the window."

Alistair rushed to the window and lifted the glass. "That won't work. There're more Hunters waiting outside."

"Dammit." Kobe ran his palms over his buzz cut. "Do we sacrifice one of us? I mean, I'll volunteer."

"You will not," Zahra spat, clutching his wrist, just to make sure.

Eden recalled what Kai said about pures and adults. They couldn't dare send Harper or Deacon, and offering Kai was a definite no. Zahra and Kobe were both nineteen, adults. She rasped, "I'll do it. I'll run out through them, distract them while you all escape."

"Edie?" Kai breathed her name, so light he was barely heard.

"You're not doing that," Lacey demanded, finding a place by Eden's side.

Exasperated, Eden sighed. "What else is there?"

"Your powers. You can create a portal."

Eden blinked a few times, staring at her mother. "You know about that?"

Lacey nodded, a sad smile crossing her face. She led Eden to the wall opposite the window. Resting her palm against the dull wallpaper, she said, "Use this to stabilize it."

Looking over her shoulder, Eden found everyone gazing at her hopefully. The fact she'd only ever created a portal big enough to fit her own body through didn't matter to them. They knew she could do it. And somehow, that was enough for her to believe it, too.

The handle wobbled, soon followed by pounding against the wooden door. Alistair ran to the door and pressed his hands against it as it shook. Kai lifted the steel bed frame and ripped it into pieces as though it was paper. He threw the broken frame to Alistair, who chocked it against the door. Deacon rushed to help, standing behind the door and creating a shield.

Every time a Hunter hit the door, Deacon's shield flickered. He shot a glance over his shoulder to Eden. "Those freaking clasps make my powers weak. If you're gonna do something, do it now."

"Eden?" Lacey urged. "Everyone needs you to focus."

Eden faced the wall. Remembering her brief training, she zoned out of the distracting surroundings and brought her attention to her hands. She created a circle shape with her fingers and thumb and rested her wrists against the wall. The pounding on the door became muffled as she closed her eyes and thought about New Sanctuary. The rolling field and homely barns, the stretching forest and the cool watering hole. Taking a deep breath, she focused intently on the field in front of the food hall. She imagined the chilly breeze rustling the grass and tickling her face. The distant sounds of laughter and friends drifted through the air. A feeling of home and safety and togetherness seeped into her heart and flowed through her body.

"New Sanctuary," she whispered to herself.

When she opened her eyes, a purple spark glowed brightly between her hands. She took a deep breath and opened her hands, widening the reach. A portal appeared in front of her, like a small oval door inside of the wall. Night stars and darkened grass waited on the other side.

The door burst open and Eden spun around. Three Hunters charged through, knocking Alistair to the ground. Her connection to the portal dimmed.

She watched Deacon help Alistair up and drag him behind Eden. Kai, Harper, and the twins hurried to block the Hunters from breaching any farther. Kai pushed Harper behind him and she toppled back into Lacey's arms.

"Eden!" Lacey screamed, holding tight to a squirming Harper. "Open the portal. Now!"

Eden turned back. The portal had reduced to half the size. She slammed a hand against the wall at one side of the portal's edge and ran to the corner of the room, dragging her hand along the wallpaper. The portal followed her, opening up the space. As though using her telekinetic ability, she flicked her wrist up. The portal expanded, reaching from the floor to the ceiling. It covered half the wall.

Lacey pulled Harper through first. Deacon, Zahra, and Kobe were next, jumping through shoulder to shoulder. Alistair stopped by Eden's side as though strategically placing himself in between her and Kai.

She stretched around him to see Kai fighting the

men alone. Two more Hunters had joined the initial three. Blackened eyes and smirking mouths surrounded him. One lone Nephilim in the middle of five Hunters.

Kai slammed his palm into one Hunter's chest and they toppled out of the room, rolling along the mezzanine. Another jumped on Kai's back, bearing rotten teeth as he growled. As hands circled around Kai's neck, he twisted and reached over, yanking the Hunter off and throwing him across the room. Seeing Kai's unmatched strength, the remaining three began getting nervous, hesitating before approaching. One removed a pistol from his holster, pointing it at Kai's chest.

Eden knew that it couldn't hurt him, not lethally anyway. But the sight still sent shivers racing down her spine. She clawed her fingers, ready to send them flying, but as she was about to use her power, Alistair pushed her through the portal.

The shock movement dazed her for a moment, blinking as she peered back through the open portal. Alone, Kai kept fighting. He slammed his hand around the gun pointed at him, tearing it from the Hunter's grip. He snapped the gun in two, giving the three Hunter's a menacing grin.

In an act of either bravery or stupidity, one of the Hunter's lunged at Kai, a war cry expelling from his gut. Before he even made contact, Kai clutched the man's collar and lifted him off the ground. Behind him, another Hunter crept forward, a glowing clasp in his hand. He reached, tucking the clasp into the hand of the man Kai was holding.

Eden jolted, stepping to run back through the portal, but she couldn't move, her wrist being held by Alistair. Stretching as close as she could, she willed her power to work through the portal.

The Hunters movements slowed but using two separate abilities drained her energy. As she fell to her knees, the portal started reducing in size. Slowly it retracted, threatening to trap Kai inside.

He held the Hunter, lifting his body up as far as his arm could stretch. His face had an expression that would make it seem he enjoyed his power, taking his time to revel in it, unaware of the clasp edging its way to his wrist. Kai seemed to enjoy it so much that Eden thought he might decide to stay there, or maybe he didn't even realize the rest of them had escaped and were waiting for him.

Struggling to hold on to the Hunters while keeping the portal open. It felt like she was carrying two hundred pounds on her back. But there was no way she'd leave Kai. She'd keep going until she passed out. Voice-shaking, Eden cried, "Kai!"

A sharp pain ached deep between her shoulder-blades. And as she thrust her last drop of energy, two wings burst open. They were large but the pressure instantly lifted. She felt stronger, more in control.

Eden let out an almighty cry, pushing her powers beyond their limits. The Hunters froze mid-strike. In their subdued state, Kai snapped out of his warrior mode. Noticing Eden waiting on the other side of the portal, he bolted for it, zipping through the small space just before it shrunk into nothingness. Finally, Eden could let go, collapsing to the ground.

29

Kai

It was quiet, aside from the sound of a collective catching of breath. Kai hunched over on his knees, feeling the coarse grass between his fingers. His bruised knuckles were visible even in the low light.

"We got her!" Zahra boomed, rushing for Harper.

"We got her!" Kobe repeated a little louder.

The twins erupted into laughter as they swept their arms around Harper. Deacon stood back with his arms crossed, the smallest of smiles made barely visible by the moonlight. He glanced at Kai, giving a stoic nod.

Kai jumped to his feet and took a few steps to stop by Eden, who was kneeling on the ground, staring at the sky. Her eyes drifted from the stars to his face and a sweet smile grew. She teased, "Took your time."

He let his fingers rake through the streak in her hair and mouthed, "Thank you."

There was a brief desire to drop to his knees and take her in his arms. She'd never used both teleportation and telekinesis at the same time before.

Watching her use her powers and knowing how hard that would have been, made him admire her even more. If that was even possible.

"Kai?" Harper's sweet voice broke his enchantment with Eden.

Tearing himself away, he ran for his sister. Since his memory returned, this was the moment he'd feared would never happen, getting her home safe. He wrapped his arms around her, picked her up off the ground, and spun in a circle. Her laughter echoed through the wind.

Lights flicked on inside the living barn. Not long after, the door opened and a groggy Wyatt peered out into the night. When his eyes adjusted, he rushed back inside and Kai heard a muffled cry of Annika's name.

Within a moment, Annika was running outside straight for the group. When her eyes found Harper, she let out an uncharacteristic "Ha!" She brushed past Kai, pushing him out of the way, and took Harper's face in her hands. She twisted Harper's head around to check on the color. "You're okay?"

Harper nodded, smiling at Kai. "Mm-hmm, he arrived before they could trade me for extraction."

Annika's face turned serious, and she dropped her hands. "You silly girl, I told you not to follow him."

"Aww, come on. Don't be so harsh," Kai interjected. "She takes after her brother, it isn't so bad is it, Annie?"

His older sister was quiet for a second, she stared at the ground, her chin tilted toward him. "You haven't called me that since we were kids."

Kai swallowed and gave a nervous smile. "I thought maybe it was time to start again."

"Yeah?" She looked up then, her eyes boring into his soul. "I think it's probably too late for that."

Zahra cleared her throat. "Okaaaay, I think this is a sibling moment. You all right, Eden? Let's get some rest."

Kai's head was low as he watched Eden struggle to stand. Again, an urge to comfort her swept over him. He resisted. There were a few things he needed to say to Annika. Eden leaned against Alistair for support, and along with Deacon and the twins, they made their way inside.

"You can go, too," Annika commanded, staring at Harper.

"But I..." Harper started but the glare from her sister was enough to obey. She frowned and ran to the barn.

When everyone was out of earshot, Annika spun back to Kai. "I don't even want to look at you. How could you do that?"

"How could I what?" Kai defended. "Save our sister?"

Disbelief flashed across her eyes. Annika lifted her cheekbones, the moon highlighting their sharp edges. "Put Deacon's life in danger."

It was Deacon's choice. Kai couldn't understand how she didn't see that. He never made anyone do anything they didn't want to. Did she really believe that everything was his fault?

Annika rubbed her hands over her bare arms and turned her gaze upward. The vulnerability in her face in that moment reminded Kai of the big sister she used to be. He asked, "What happened between us?"

Eyes still above, she grimaced and shook her head. "You know why."

"New York?"

"Yes," she hissed. "And Harper. And..." Her voice lowered. "Maddox."

"Maddox?" Kai was taken aback. "You blame me for that?"

Annika lowered her head and met Kai's question with a shiver. Glimmering in the corner of her eye was a tear, threatening to spill. She sniffed and turned away, too proud to show her brother any weakness.

Kai knew that her heightened animosity she'd

carried started with the New York incident. But it only just made sense to him why that was. It was the moment Maddox was taken from her. It broke her. He ripped off his jacket and held it out. "Here, take this."

"I don't want your pity, Malakai." Her tone was a little less spiteful than normal. Without looking, she pushed his hands back.

"I'm sorry," Kai said, putting his jacket back on. "Is that what you want? Someone to blame? Fine, blame me. I'll take it. It's my fault."

Annika shook her head, still refusing to show her face. She remained silent for a while, content to stand in the cold with her sorrow. Finally, she faced him, a distinct numbness to her glare. "I won't need to blame you for anything, brother. If you just do what I tell you. I forbid you from leaving this place again."

"You forbid me?" Kai was shocked at first, but soon anger rose. "Sister, give me a break. I'm eighteen, you have no control over me. You never have."

"Listen to my words." Annika met his gaze, a renewed fire burning in her eyes. "If you leave, you are not welcome back."

Kai stepped away and scoffed. "This is what I don't understand. Our father's warrior grace burns me, doesn't it burn you? Don't you want justice?"

"Yes, but I don't have death's daughter as a sidekick. Chaos follows you."

"That's not fair and you know it." Kai knew she'd meant to hurt him with that remark. But now he knew the truth, he could see right through her. Annika didn't hate Eden; she was jealous that Kai had someone when she didn't.

"Is everything okay?" The sound of Eden's voice made Kai's heart do a double-beat.

Annika rolled her eyes. "Speak of the devil."

For the third time, a rush of protective instinct flowed through him. This time, he succumbed. He took Eden by the hand and said, "Not really. Annika forbids us from leaving New Sanctuary."

Annika moaned. "I forbid you from getting caught and having your mind wiped again."

The conversation was going in circles. Kai was over it, and he was over his sister's cruel stare. He didn't want to argue anymore, especially with Eden around. She made him happier, less inclined to punch and more inclined to hug.

"I'm tired," Kai stated. He squeezed Eden's hand and led her toward the barn. Loud enough for Annika to hear, he said, "Don't listen to her, she's just angry and bitter."

Eden

"Happy Birthday, Edie."

The words were accompanied by a gentle shoulder shake. Eden pried her eyes open to see Kai kneeling over her with a gigantic smile. He waved a tiny box in front of her face.

Eden smiled and sat up. She glanced around the room to see most people were still sleeping. Taking the box from Kai, she whispered, "You didn't have to get me anything."

"I've missed the last six birthdays," he stated, dropping the box into her hand.

She tugged at the blue ribbon around the box and lifted the lid. Inside was a transparent vial with glowing blue liquid. Eden gasped. It was the vial they found in her father's lab, created to bring Kai's memories back sooner. The last drop of memory serum that remained from when the Hunters ransacked her house.

"I couldn't," Eden's voice cracked, not quite a

whisper anymore. "It's the only one left."

Kai nodded. "Exactly. If we get extracted again, I want you to have it. I've already had my share... it's only fair."

A moan rumbled from the bed beside Eden's. Deacon chided, "Ugh, you two make me sick with your declarations of love. You're even rhyming. What's next? Sonnets?"

He swiped the pillow from Eden's mat and threw it on his face, crossing his arms over the top. A moment later, he muffled, "Happy birthday, Eden."

"Thanks, Deacon," she replied, tapping the pillow on his face. She carefully returned the lid to the box and slid it under the covers. "Let's hope neither of us need it."

Near the door of the barn, Raphael's descendants were busy fussing over Harper, giving her hugs and asking her excited questions about her capture. It was their turn to make breakfast, but going by the distraction, it would be another half an hour before anything was served.

Kai climbed over his bed and rustled through his belongings. Pulling out a towel, he whispered, "Wanna go for an early morning swim before breakfast?"

Aware of Deacon within earshot and his tendency to complain about missing out, Eden threw her thumb over her shoulder. "Should we invite him?"

Smiling, Kai shook his head. "Not this time. Just us."

The thought of swimming sounded, well, not that great in this temperature, but the prospect of spending more alone time with him, sent her mind whirring. Did he have a plan to save the other Nephilim? Or maybe, he wanted to kiss her again. Eden bounded to her bag at the end of the bed and gathered her shorts and tee to swim in. As she followed Kai to the door, she gazed back at Deacon.

The pillow covering his face shifted, and a voice

called from beneath it. "Didn't want to go anyway!"

Water lapped at the edges of the lake. Eden stood close, her bare feet hanging over the edge. She dipped her toes in, bracing for the chill. But instead, it was warm.

"Oh," she said, stepping in. "I thought it would be cold."

Kai laughed. "I think it's some kind of natural hot spring. Either that or you're a wimp."

"Oh yeah?" Eden said, pushing him playfully.

He used the forward motion and dove in. When he emerged he squirted water out his mouth like a fountain. "Remember Lake Louise?"

Pouting, Eden let herself sink into the warm water. "Lake Louise ices over, you can't call me a wimp for not wanting to swim in that!"

Kai gave a wry smile and flicked his fingers in her direction, splashing tiny drops of water over her face. Before she had the chance to retaliate, he took a breath and disappeared under water. Eden watched him beneath the surface, swimming closer to her.

Giggling, she waded out of his reach. As he approached, she closed her mouth in anticipation. He clutched at her waist and dragged her under.

Water lapped over her eyes, distorting her vision of him. Yet somehow, as clear as crystal, she could see his bright blue irises shining in delight. The moment brought her back to a time and place—before New Sanctuary, before extraction, where memories weren't fractured and their race wasn't threatened. Back to Lumeria, when they were six...

Her and Kai, young and innocent, swam near the jetty. Annika over-looked them, dangling her feet into the water, carving her initials into the wooden beams. Kai stood on top of a cliff, nearly twenty meters above the lake.

"I've told you," twelve-year-old Annika warned. "If you break your wings, I'm not going back to the Healers with you for the third time this month. That's just embarrassing."

A bubble formed in Eden's stomach. With her most serious voice, she called up to Kai, "Don't worry. I'll take you."

Annika grinned and shook her head. "You are too cute, Eden—"

The ground shook, sending ripples across the lake. Then, the noise followed—a rumble that seemed to go on for ages, mixed with blood-curdling screams and intermittent pops.

Annika, Kai, and Eden flew to the city. They'd never experienced violence before and were young enough to believe they'd be safe in their districts. Landing alongside death soon changed their thoughts. But it was too late.

Most of them were taken, locked up in a chamber five floors high. Cages mounted upon cages, like rats in a lab. Some of them managed to evade capture, Chamuel's descendants mostly. Using their shielding abilities, they grabbed babies or the elderly and ran to other parts of the globe. It was Deacon's brother, Maddox, who took Harper, only two years old.

At six years old, Eden wasn't aware of the future, how the cycle of madness would continue on until there were only a small number of Nephilim remaining. She was small and sassy and never dreamed of war. Yet, she was taken, along with her people.

At six years old, she watched those older than fourteen die from extraction, their bodies laid to waste on the chamber floor. And, still grieving, she was put inside a glass cage of her own with tubes and needles invading her body.

Just six years old...

Eden surfaced, her eighteen-year-old lungs gasping for air. She tried to breathe but all she could do was scream. Panic-stricken she scrambled out of the water, digging her fingers into soil. Her wings rolled out, falling by her side in arches.

"Edie?" Kai asked, but even his voice couldn't help calm her.

She lifted off the ground.

"Eden?" Kai tried again, running beneath her as she rose.

Staring at him with tear-filled eyes, she cried, "It was our home."

Realization visibly hit him. His face fell. "I know." He reached up as she hovered above him and took her hand.

Eden wanted to stream to the clouds, escape the new memory torturing her mind. She could find somewhere to hide, pretend none of it happened, live as a human. As she inched higher, Kai tugged on her hand.

"We'll fix it," he urged. "You and me. I promise."

They'd fix it? Guilt hit her. She could escape, run away and find someplace to live in secret, but she could never outrun the memories. Or the knowledge that her people were in trouble.

She retracted her wings and fell into his arms, sobbing. "Every moment that I remember, hurts more than the last."

"Let it happen." Kai squeezed her tighter. "Don't be afraid of the memories, you're stronger than them. Surrendering to the unknown might sound weak, but, in fact, it is the opposite. To face the past with unblinking eyes is one of the strongest things you can ever do. And you'll survive it. I know this because you're still here."

A glowing light shined on the shadows hiding in her mind and the lingering fog lifted. Every missing piece, once a blank void, flooded with color, vivid and bright. Her life was no longer a puzzle but a whole picture, clear in her mind.

Eden's heart burned as she pulled out of Kai's embrace. His eyes circled her face, and in the aqua, she saw rolling fields of green grass, she saw laughter and companionship. She saw Alistair call them for supper. She saw her friends, Zahra and Kobe, Deacon, Wyatt, and baby Harper, as they sat around the lake eating homemade chocolate and showing off their powers. She saw herself and her friends open portals to different parts of the world. They spied on humans as she dreamed about being old enough to help them. She saw their home being attacked, shields lowered and their serenity erased. She saw heartache and pain and separation. But she also saw comfort and protection and friendship, a future. Hope.

She wanted that again, she'd die for them all to have that again.

Kai looked down, a soft smile lighting his face. His thumb smoothed across her palm. "There you are. I've missed you, Edie."

"I remember everything," she said, tears in her eyes, yet somehow lighter. "I've missed you, too."

He placed his hands on either side of her face and his eyes dropped to her lips. Without one second passing, he leaned forward, pressing his mouth against hers. Heart racing, Eden complied, melting into him, letting his caramel-tasting lips caress hers.

It was different from their first kiss when they were ten and wanted to know what it felt like. It was innocent back then, full of wonder and trust. This kiss was more. It was tender and hungry at once, full of passion and wanting and stirred a longing in her heart to be closer, to never let go.

His fingertips dug into her skull as he kissed her

deeper, a guttural moan rumbling in the back of his throat. The noise sent warmth from her heart throughout her body. She lifted her hands to his damp, bare chest and let her fingers settle along the dips of his muscles.

Coming up for air, they rested their foreheads together. Kai's breath was shaking. "Tell me what you know, tell me who you are."

"I'm a Nephilim. I can move things with my mind. I can create portals and teleport. My name is Eden and I'm the daughter of Azrael, and..." she faltered, breaking their eye contact for a moment. She felt his hands, strong and sure against her cheeks, willing her to look up. And so she did. "And, I'm yours."

Kai shook his head and clasped her shoulders. "No, Edie. You have it wrong. You don't belong to me." He winced as he clutched her tighter, bringing her so close that her ear was beside his mouth. He whispered, "I... am yours."

Eden

Eden couldn't walk fast enough. She was too excited and terrified all at the same time. So many memories, so much to take in.

Kai jogged behind her as she ran across the field of New Sanctuary. Every person there, she knew, she remembered. All of them had a place in her heart.

Yet, there were also many more faces, all of them gone. Some dead. Some in cages. Some missing.

She slowed her pace, trying to keep up with all the people that sped through her mind like a movie reel on a fast-forward loop. One person, specifically, stopped her dead in her tracks. Those soulful gray irises, the long flowing brown hair. The way they touched her, taught her, lied to her.

Her mother. Lacey wasn't just hiding Eden's secrets; she was hiding her own.

Eden stormed into the food hall, searching the sea of faces for one in particular. But she wasn't there. In fact, Eden couldn't remember seeing her since they escaped Nancy's.

"I'm starving, too," Kai said right behind her, unaware of her epiphany. With his hands on her waist, he guided her to the serving tray, weaving her around Wyatt and Jia, and stopped at the end of the line.

"Wait!" Eden shimmied out of his hold. "I need to ask Wyatt something."

"Okay," Kai called after her. "I'll get you some food."

Eden would have teased him about how out of character that was, but her mother's face plagued her mind. She needed answers. Interrupting Jia and Wyatt, she blurted, "Where's Lacey?"

"Lacey?" Wyatt frowned. "Who's that?"

Confused, Eden turned to Jia, awaiting her response.

Jia's eyes were dreamy and sparkling as she gazed over Eden's shoulder. Eden shot a glance at what she was looking at. It was Deacon, obviously. He was leaning against a wooden beam, watching people while picking at his teeth. His eyes drifted to Jia and he flashed a wink. Eden turned back and when she saw Jia's cheeks burning red, she gave up on asking her anything.

"Forget it," Eden muttered, searching the room again.

"Are you all right?" Wyatt asked, placing a strong hand on her shoulder.

Eden spotted Alistair in the corner, his spoon splashing in and out of his oatmeal. "I'm fine," she spat, running for her dad. When she reached him, she slammed her hands on the table, breathless. "Where's mom?"

Alistair looked up from his bowl, sadness clouding his eyes. "You know about her, don't you?"

Eden gasped. Something about his expression gave her pause. "Where..." Eden hesitated. "Has she gone?"

Shrugging, Alistair returned to his food. Despondently, he said, "Wherever it is that they go."

Her legs couldn't move fast enough. Eden hightailed it out of the barn. Face upward, she screamed, "Moooom?"

A sparrow flitted above her, she watched it land on the top of a tree at the edge of the forest. The morning was almost warm, and the clear blue sky was occupied by one lone wispy cloud.

"Mom?" she cried again, running barefoot along the grass.

When she reached the forest, she stopped and turned around. Across the field, two barns and a small garage sat, the small buildings hidden amongst the trees and mountains and lake. It was a humble hideout. Not Lumeria, though. Not a place between Heaven and Earth where the Archangels could visit whenever they liked.

Eden wiped a tear, just thinking about the sacrifice her mother made. A whimper fell from her lips. Once more, she tried...

"Azrael?"

A gentle hand cupped her shoulder. "I'm here."

Eden spun around to see Lacey smiling. "Mom?" Another tear fell. "You gave up your powers to be with me?"

Lacey slid her fingertips down Eden's arm and grabbed her hands. Squeezing, she answered, "It was worth every second."

"Where did you go?"

A sadness fell over Lacey. "I cannot be here. Not amongst everyone. It's not the way we do things."

Eden thought about her years at Lumeria. Archangels would never visit them; most children never got the chance to meet their parent. She was lucky in that aspect; Azrael visited her once when she was five and showing signs of telekinetic abilities. It was unlike all the other descendants, who could only teleport and create portals. And something else was different, her wings. They weren't black. They were both black and white.

Eden pushed hard into the memory, trying to recall the reason why. But even with her full past being known to her, a five-year-old mind may have the perspective wrong. She just felt like an anomaly.

"You told me I was special," Eden said vaguely. "When you came to Lumeria."

"You were... are special," Lacey confirmed.

Blinking, Eden gazed into her mother's eyes. "Why?"

Hesitating, Lacey's pupils dilated, her gray eyes darkening. Then, she rolled her shoulders and two obsidian wings expanded around her. They looked velvet to touch and even in their folded state, were larger than any other Eden had seen. With pained eyes, she said, "Show me yours."

With a shaking breath, Eden stood up straight and let her wings unfurl. She let her gaze drift from their base, black as night, all the way to their tips, white as snow.

Lacey sighed. "They are perfect."

Eden stared at her mother. "Is that why I'm special? Because of a birth defect?" The thought made her sick. She was different, yes, but not special. No more than every other Nephilim from Lumeria. Eden thought of Jia, her mother's descendant who'd been in captive for twelve years. "You have other children, you know."

If Eden's words hurt Lacey, she didn't show it. She only nodded. "They're all dead."

"Not Wyatt," Eden huffed, refusing to feel guilty for her accusation. "Not Jia. Not all your other grandchildren still in captive."

"I have no power here on Earth, it's why we began having children in the first—"

"Don't give me that," Eden cut her off. "It's an

excuse and you know it. Do you and the other Archangels even care about the genocide of their precious race?"

"Enough!" Lacey scolded. She rested her hand on a tree. The movement gave way to a shimmer behind her.

Eden peered around. About three meters to the back of the tree, a door-sized portal revealed a white cobbled road surrounded by glass skyscrapers. "I thought you couldn't use your powers here?"

Lacey glanced over her shoulder. "I can't. This portal is connected to Heaven. It's how I bring people there."

Heaven? Eden stepped to the side, trying to catch a better glimpse.

Lacey clutched Eden's wrist. "Don't get too close, Eden. Death comes to those who step through."

Stopping, Eden sighed. Maybe her anger was misdirected. Her mother's job was important. Where was time to save the world, when she was bringing people out of it? "How did people get to Heaven while you were with me?"

"I had help from someone who thought your safety was paramount to the survival of our race. Who agreed that I should be with you until you remembered." Lacey inhaled sharply. "Listen, Eden. I have to go home now. My right of leave ended the moment you got your memories back. But hear me when I say, I believe in you. You are special. You have more power within you than anyone on this Earth. Trust yourself. Surprise yourself."

Lacey tugged Eden close to her breast. She held her for a moment, then pushed her away, turning hastily to the portal. Without another word, she stepped through, closing the portal behind her.

The departure left Eden feeling empty. Lacey's coldness wasn't rare. Over the last six years, Eden had found more comfort in Alistair, than in her distant mother. She seemed to only show interest during their nightly interrogation. But still, a little piece of her had hoped that since the connection between them was of blood, not obligation, there'd be a deeper bond.

Eden sauntered back to the food hall, swallowing the lump forming in her throat. She'd have to deal with the fact that Archangels didn't care about their sires. It was just the way it was. After all, her own mother didn't even wish her a Happy Birthday.

She found Kai and her friends gathered at their usual table. Sliding in beside Kai, she sighed long and loud.

The tap of bare feet along floorboards was followed by Jia taking a seat opposite Deacon. She waved to Eden. "I hear it's your birthday?"

Eden gave a slight nod.

"Happy birthday, Eeeds," Kobe cried. He raised his arms and his brows, the crescent scar above his eye dancing with exuberance.

The sound and sight lifted her a little.

"Ack!" Zahra bounded up. Behind her, the chair crashed to the ground from the rushed movement. Ignoring it, she ran around the table, her arms open wide.

Eden watched Zahra race for her, an excitement rising within. Zahra wrapped her arms across Eden from behind and embraced her tightly. "I can't believe I forgot. Happy birthday, girl."

"It's okay," Eden replied. She clutched onto Zahra's arms, making sure she felt the appreciation. "I forgot a whole life, so I can forgive you for one date."

Zahra guffawed and made her way back around the table. She picked up her chair and returned to her breakfast, chowing down on oatmeal as though it was ice cream. Eden's stomach grumbled, and she threw an arm across her belly, darting her eyes around to see who heard. Kai gave her a side-eye. With a guilt-ridden face, he removed the spoon from his mouth and dropped it into the half-eaten oats in front of him. To the side of the bowl, was another—empty. He pushed what was meant to be her breakfast over.

His willingness to give up food made her smile. She waved her hand at him. "It's okay, I'm not hungry."

Kai's eyes turned to slits. He glanced at the arm across her stomach and back at the bowl. Smacking his lips together, he pushed the bowl closer to her. "Are you okay?"

Eden looked around at her friends. Their eager yet concerned faces, waiting for her reply. They'd always been there. In Lumeria, in New Sanctuary, even Zahra and Kobe in New York. They were her family, the ones who had always been there.

"I'm good. Really good." Eden let her hand fall on top of Kai's. Immediately, he twisted his hand and thread his fingers through hers. "I'm so happy we're all together."

Eden

After breakfast, Wyatt grabbed a chair from the table behind them and slammed it down in between Eden and Kai. "No training today, folks. We'll call it a day of celebration. Because Harper was saved." He pointed between Jia and Eden. "And that you've both got your full memories back. And also, of course..." He placed a bag in front of Eden, his white streak falling over his eyes. "Eden's birthday."

Eden stared at it and then him. "You didn't have to —"

"Shhh," Kai hushed. "You've said that already today, just accept it."

Wyatt threw his thumb and pointed it at Kai. "He's wise. Well, most of the time. Okay, maybe not wise, but he's... right. Just open it."

Eden didn't realize how much she hated being made a fuss of. With all eyes on her, she smiled shyly and cracked the top of the paper bag open.

"Hurry up," Deacon moaned. "It's only your

birthday for one day."

Ignoring him, Eden tilted the bag so she could see inside. A foot-long black feather sat proudly inside. Eden lifted it out. She twisted the quill between her fingers and the barn's fairy lights bounced off the tip. It felt like velvet and silk melted together. She knew who it belonged to even before he said anything.

"It's Azrael's," Wyatt explained. "My mother gave it to me before Lumeria was attacked, and I found it again in the rubble a few years ago."

"You've been back there?" Zahra asked.

Wyatt nodded. "Do not recommend."

Kobe stared at the feather, eyes glistening with wonderment. "How the heck did your mom get an Archangel feather?"

"Apparently, Azrael visited Lumeria once. Very briefly and only to our sector. Not many people saw her. Anyway, she gave it to my mom, said it was a part of her. To hold on to it whenever she needed comfort."

Eden ran her finger down the side of the feather. It bent over, soft and pliable, and then bounced back into position. Touching it, knowing it was Lacey's, sent her mind to the last six years.

To the way Lacey's eyes gleamed whenever Eden recalled a new memory. The way she stayed with Eden in her room, wiping sweat from her brow, when she was sick with the flu. Her excitement at seeing Eden win first prize in a shoe design competition. The smell of baking cakes and cookies, spreading through the house, along with her voice as it sang advertisement jingles from the television. Their trips to Vermont and days spent skiing on the slopes.

Maybe the Archangels did care about their descendants. Even if it was only to make sure their legacy lived on. Eden's whole body buzzed with the notion. She had been looking to her mom for all the wrong things. She wanted warmth and comfort and family, but she already had a family amongst her friends and Alistair.

Of course, Lacey cared, but that wasn't what mattered. What truly mattered was the thing she'd given Eden—the desire to heal the world.

Eden looked around the food hall at all the Nephilim, scared and in hiding. They weren't meant for this. Lacey said the Archangels had children to be able to use their powers on Earth.

"Thank you," Eden said to Wyatt, rising. Still glancing around the room, she leaned over and wrapped her arms around his neck. "You're the best, cuz."

Moving to Kai, she tapped his shoulder and lowered her voice. "Meet me outside in five?"

He nodded. The way his eyes danced around her face made her heart warm. He'd always tried to do what their parents had wanted. And she'd always agreed with him.

Together, they were going to step into what they were always meant to be. Earth Angels.

But first, she needed to speak with Alistair; she needed to have his support.

Eden gave one more scan of the hall, and not being able to find him there, she ran across to the living barn. Alistair was sitting on a sofa by the back window, golden morning sun shining across his face. His head was tilted toward the light, eyes closed as though in a different world.

Walking across the room, she made a stop by her bed and retrieved the vial Kai gave to her earlier. She shoved the vial into her jeans pocket as she dodged the mats to the ladder. She climbed up to the mezzanine lounge area and threw herself onto the sofa with a thud.

Alistair jolted and opened his eyes. When he realized it was Eden, he sighed. "Happy birthday, sweetheart. I didn't get a chance to tell you before, I got you a gift but it was in the apartment—"

"It doesn't matter," Eden burst, throwing her arms around him. She squeezed him tight before moving back.

"What was that for?"

"For being my father. And not just looking after me and feeding me and making sure I didn't go off the teenager rails. But for being a dad, when you didn't have to."

Alistair smiled and craned his face to the sun. "Do you remember Lumeria?"

She did. He was their watcher. Every sector was governed by one. Watchers were lower Angels, with no ability other than being gracious and kind. He'd been with her every step of the way. "I remember."

Turning back to her, Alistair said, "They wanted to separate you from Kai, they thought the two of you together brought more harm than good. I put my hand up to take you in, there was no other option in my mind. I love you, Eden. To me, you are my child. You all are."

"I know," Eden said. "I love you, too."

Alistair nodded then grinned larger than before. "So, what have you got planned for the day?"

"Oh, you know." Eden placed her elbow on the sofa's back and rested her head in her hand. "Just a small revolution."

Frowning, Alistair leaned closer. His eyes flitted between hers as if trying to see if she was joking or not. He must have seen something to confirm his suspicions. "How about a game of Twister? Or we can bake a caramel cake? I mean, I don't know how your mother made them so delicious, but we can try?"

A familiar father/daughter feeling washed over her. Eden tilted her head and glowered. "I can't just stay here and pretend everything is fine."

Alistair removed his glasses and pinched the bridge of his nose. He moaned, "Eden."

"Dad, please. This isn't what we are made for." She

circled her arm. "We have to go and save those who are still in captive. I feel it in my soul, it aches every part of me. Have you forgotten Lumeria? The joy, the laughter, the community? I'm going to save them; I'm going to bring our people home."

"Not yet, you're not." Alistair's tone dropped. Almost immediately after, he seemed shocked at his own outburst. He clutched Eden's bicep. "I'm sorry, I know they're not the words you want to hear. But it's about Kai."

He glanced around the room, making sure no one was in earshot. Hunching over, his low voice rumbled, "No one has survived more than three extractions. He was the first. He may not have even gotten his memory back without help."

"Your help?" Eden touched the vial in her back pocket.

"Yes." Alistair frowned. "And all my work is gone, the Hunters made sure of that."

She grasped the vial and folded her hand around it. Kai gave it to her, just in case they came to any trouble and she'd need her memory back. But somehow, it felt selfish to keep it. If she were to save her people, she needed to do it with one result in mind —to set her kind free.

There was a sacrificial notion to that intention. It wasn't her or them. But if it had to be, she knew the choice she'd make.

Holding her hand between them, she splayed her fingers. "Can you recreate it from this?"

Mouth agape, Alistair took the vial. "How did you get this?"

"I found it in your lab."

Bringing it to the sunlight, Alistair's eyes sparkled through the blue liquid. "Yes, I think I will be able to use it." He dropped his hands to his lap. "But, Eden, this is all that's left. I won't be able to recreate it immediately. I'll need a lab and time. If you run out of here like cowboys, I won't be able to use it on you and everyone else."

Eden knew that. And the decision had already ignited a spark inside her heart, there was no turning back from it now. She'd give up her life, her memories, if it meant the Nephilim were free. "Then, don't use it on me. Take the vial and produce more, enough to restore everyone's memories and abilities."

Wincing, Alistair shook his head. "I can't condone it. You're risking your life."

"I know. But that's the choice, isn't it? Those Nephilim caught in the chambers; they don't have any choice."

Alistair stroked his thumb along Eden's jawline. "You're too much, Eden. Don't you get it? It's a suicide mission."

She nodded. "I said, I know."

Determination drove her. Nothing he or Annika or Wyatt could say would change her mind. She was going to save the Nephilim or die trying.

Kai

"Hey, man." Kobe plonked himself on the ground. "Want company?"

"Sure," Kai said, twiddling a strand of grass around his fingers. He glanced at the barn, half expecting Eden to be walking over with that innocuous smile of hers.

He knew why she wanted to meet him. Now that her full memory was back, as always, she wanted to do something to save her kind. And, as always, so did he. But this time, there was a tiny flicker of doubt circling his mind.

Annika.

Kai hated that she didn't trust him. Didn't she know that he was strong enough to take out five Hunters all on his own? If they all worked together, they'd be unstoppable. What was she so afraid of?

Kai could sense Kobe's eyes on him. "What?"

"You're keen to do something, aren't you? Something big."

Sighing, Kai lifted his knees and rested his arms over them. Still twiddling with the strand of grass, he said, "I guess it's just who I am. But no one else agrees with me."

"I do." Kobe tugged at the grass in front of him, mindlessly twisting a strand like Kai.

"You and Eden. What an army." Kai's voice was thick with sarcasm.

"It is, you know. With Deacon and Zahra, too. We're a force." Kobe raised one eyebrow as his lip curled into a smirk.

Kai thought back to Annika's snarling words. How could you put Deacon's life in danger? He'd risked his friend's life for his sister's. Who was he to decide whose life was worth more than another's?

From outside, he could hear the giggles and fawning over Harper. While they basked in their triumph of bringing Harper home, Kai was stuck in his own head, wondering if Annika was right the whole time. This time, the risk worked out, but if Deacon was caught...

Kai dropped the piece of grass. "It was a bad decision, bringing Deacon... even bringing you and Zahra. He's a pure and you're nineteen, adults. If they extract you, they won't care if you'll die. As long as they get their grace—"

"Death is the risk of war," Kobe mused, eyes drifting above.

"I wish we didn't have to think like this." Kai shook his head and lay back down.

He'd often open his eyes in the morning, hoping he'd awaken to the real world and finding out everything for the last twelve years had been all a bad dream. "Sometimes, if you look at the sky in the right way, it's easy to pretend you're in Lumeria."

Kobe lay down. Both of them in silence for a while.

"Grab as many as you can," a gruff voice rasped nearby.

Kai sat up. As soon as he caught sight of who it was, his heart fell to his feet and back up again. A Hunter. Not one though, at least two dozen. All charging through a portal in the field.

Kobe jumped to his feet, looking down at Kai for direction. "What do we do?"

"Harper!" Kai commanded, standing. "Go find her, protect her."

As Kobe ran for the barns, Kai charged at the group of Hunters. Like all descendants of Michael, he was swift and agile. He stormed across the field as quiet as a ninja, reaching the Hunters before they even noticed he was coming.

Kai crashed through the middle of their line. He didn't need any weapons; his whole body was the sword. Strong. Precise. Lethal.

He threw the first Hunter he could grab. The woman flew through the air in an arch, landing twenty meters away. Startled, a nearby Hunter fumbled with his gun. When he cocked it in Kai's direction, Kai grinned and clutched the barrel, crushing the metal inside his fist. He sent the same fist onto the Hunter's face, knocking him out cold. As Kai eyed his next victim, a Hunter jumped on his back, limbs circling his neck and waist in desperation. To Kai, it was nothing more than an inconvenient disturbance. He swiveled his torso, bucking the Hunter off and sending him skidding along the ground.

The Hunters separated, all fleeing in different directions away from Kai. Some to each barn, others back in through the portal. A few shots were fired at the window on the side of the living barn and the sound of crashing glass was surpassed by screams from inside.

Kai jolted on the spot. His instinct was to follow the loudest noise but the sight of a Hunter clutching a bronze clasp caught his eye. He set his sights on the Hunter and picked up his speed.

Reaching her, Kai wrapped his arms around her shoulders, squeezing tight. The Hunter's knees buckled and Kai followed her to the ground, making sure she was down.

When he let go, however, something had shifted. Kai's power had subsided. No longer did he feel invincible, the power that surged through his muscles fizzled like a car out of gas. Lifting his hand, he saw a bronze clasp around his wrist.

The Hunter spun around, breathless. Her eyes were fogged over, black reaching out from her irises in waves. With all her might, she lifted her gun and swung it in Kai's direction. The butt of the gun thwacked across his head, sending the edges of his vision white.

A strange dizziness swept through him and he crashed to the ground. Kai blinked, willing himself to stay awake. Helpless and motionless, he felt warm blood trickle down his chin as the sound of screams echoed around him. The noise rattled inside his skull, taunting him, as though all of New Sanctuary was trapped inside his mind. He let his head fall upon the grass.

I'll just rest my eyes, he thought, convincing himself it would help him regain his strength.

"Kobe!" someone screamed as though their life depended on it.

Kai darted his eyes open to a fuzzy vision of three men heading out of a barn. Two were holding one—someone with platinum blond hair.

Head aching, Kai tilted his face, to see better. Deacon wrestled against two Hunters as they dragged him back toward the portal. Not too far behind, Kobe charged after them.

"Kobe!" Deacon screamed again. Kai could tell he was trying to open his wings and use his shield, but the clasp around his wrist was stopping him.

"No! Deacon!" Kobe puffed, tripping over his own

feet. He tumbled to the ground, knees and elbows cracking into the soil.

Kai moaned, bringing his hands up under himself. He pushed, but even his own body felt too heavy. Collapsing to the ground, he rasped out a defeated, "Come on."

He tried again, managing to shift his knees under his chest. Stopping for breath, he looked through the portal that Deacon was headed for.

Inside was dark and gray, but there was no mistaking the cage-lined wall. The cries of Nephilim trapped inside them echoed into the field, they called for help and freedom through the crack in time and space. One girl, hands clutching the bars, stared in disbelief as she watched the scene before her.

Kai's whole body shook with rage. All he could do was watch, too.

Watch the Hunters drag a pure through the portal.

Watch Deacon, become a captive.

Watch Kobe, as he jumped to his feet, shifted into a wolf, and leaped into the portal.

"No, no, no," Kai muttered as he again brought his hands under. With shaking arms he pushed himself up, a guttural cry rumbling in his throat.

On his knees, tired and weak, he studied the clasp around his wrist. Not only did it render his powers useless, but when he was struck it kept the damage human-like. How fragile humans must be. In frustration, he whacked his hand to the ground. Once. Twice. He smacked the clasp as hard as he could. Again. And again. And again.

Not even a crack.

"Malakai?" a sweet voice called out behind him.

"Harper?" he rasped as she ran into view. Relief flooded as his shaking hands sifted through her hair. "Oh my God, you're okay? You're okay!"

Noticing the clasp, she clutched his arm. Careful not to touch it, she pummeled his arm onto the ground. The soil shifted under the force and a small crack snaked its way along the rim of the clasp.

"That's it," Kai urged. "You can do it. Don't be scared to hurt me."

As she readied herself to try again, a Hunter ran around the corner. Spotting her, the Hunter grinned wildly and ran for her. In one smooth motion, Harper stood up and swung her arm. The impact knocked the Hunter out. She left him twitching on the ground and returned to Kai.

He could see the look in her eyes; of determination, of thrill. There was no doubt that she was a child of Michael. There was no doubt she was his sister.

Harper screamed as she slammed his wrist down, and Kai knew it was either his arm or the clasp that would break. Luckily, it was the clasp.

"How do you feel?" she asked, swinging his arm over her shoulders to help him up.

Wobbling to his feet, Kai replied, "A bit dizzy."

Harper glanced at the blood that curved down his face. "You're healing already. It will only take a moment until you feel like yourself again."

He didn't have a moment. Deacon and Kobe were already taken. How many more had to suffer? When would the nightmare end? When they were all dead?

By the time they got to the food hall door, he felt halfway back to normal. Turning to Harper, he pulled his arm away and stood on his own. "Find somewhere to hide."

"But, Kai, I'm strong I can help—"

Kai balled his hand into a fist and hit the side of the barn. "No arguments. I can't fight them if I'm worried about you. Just do it."

"You sound like Annika." Harper rolled her eyes. Kai glared at her until she submitted. "Ugh, fine."

He watched her until she'd made it to the edge of the forest behind the barns, and when he was satisfied that she was well out of the way, he entered the food hall.

The room was eerily quiet, save a few sniffles and whimpers.

Annika had a cluster of young Nephilim huddled in the corner, she protectively stood in front of them with her arms out, staring at the ceiling. Lionel, an Elemental Angel, crouched on the ground, his bulging muscles pushing hard against a Hunter's chest. His gaze lifted.

Eden was in the center of the room, feet hovering off the floor. Her wings were out in all their magnificent black-and-white glory. And she was glowing, her aura a mixture of the deepest blacks and the purest whites.

Above her, five Hunters were suspended on the ceiling. She kept the Hunters frozen in the air, while her eyes shot to the front window. One more Hunter, his hand clasped around Jia's neck, shuffled for the door.

Eden winced, her wrist giving the slightest of flicks and the sound of breaking bones echoed around the room. Above them, the five Hunters went limp. They hung alongside the beams, lifeless.

Kai's heart lurched. He stared at Eden waiting for some kind of reaction to what she'd just done, like grief or surprise. But the only thing he could see was fierce anger and heaviness, as though that sweet soul of hers carried the weight of the Nephilim's fate on her shoulders alone.

"Let her go," Eden demanded, staring at the Hunter who held Jia.

Her voice didn't sound normal. As if it was muffled yet magnified at the same time. Kai shuddered at the sheer sovereignty of it.

As her feet met the floor and she marched toward Jia, five bodies dropped to the ground around them. The Hunter holding Jia balked and released her, hands rising in surrender. As soon as he made one step back, Eden squinted. Her powers sent the Hunter crashing through the window and tumbling out onto the field.

Annika came charging from the back of the room, fists bloodied and ready for war. "Round them up, we need to make sure they're all accounted—"

A piercing scream came from outside.

Kai made eye contact with Annika. His feet moved before the cry ended. He knew who it was. His heart knew.

Out on the field, a few steps from the portal. A hunter had Harper by the hair and a glowing clasp wrapped her wrist.

"Kai!" she screamed. And then more sob-filled, "Annie!"

Kai's legs wouldn't go fast enough. No matter how much agility and strength he as a child of Michael could possess, in that moment, it would never be enough. Annika ran beside him, their feet stomping along the ground in unison.

Through the portal, Kai caught a glimpse of Kobe— still in wolf form—chained to a steel beam.

The Hunter dragged Harper through the portal.

Kai ran, heart pumping so fast his chest ached. The portal was so close he could smell the dank mold that lined the walls of the cages. He was going in, whether Annika liked it or not. But the fact that she was right alongside him, made him know she was thinking the same thing.

They were going in together.

In the moment it took to take one more step, the portal closed.

Wyatt stood in its place, removing the remnant that hovered in the air. He clenched his jaw, arm still held up. "I'm sorry. I had to. You were both about to do something reckless."

34

Kai

"How the hell did they find us?" Annika threw her arms in the air as she passed up and down in front of the serving tray.

Kai slumped into a chair at the nearest table and folded his arms to rest his head down.

The door creaked open and the sound of boots on the floorboards filled the room. Kai lifted his head to see Lionel enter the room. He stood next to Wyatt. "I did a perimeter check." He glanced at Eden then leaned close to whisper.

Wyatt whipped his head to Eden. "I told you to make sure you remove the remnants from the portals you create."

"I do... I did..." Eden stood at the side of the table where Kai sat. Her eyes clouded over as though straining to recall the moment they jumped through the portal from Nancy's. "I thought I did..."

"Stupid girl," Annika hissed. "Why is she even here? She ruins everything."

Kai pushed the chair back as he stood, the legs scraped along the floor. He reached over and took

Eden's hand, tugging her to stand closer to him. "The blame isn't hers. It never is. You know where the blame lies? With those Hunters. Humans. Who think they have the right to take us, to steal our grace and leave us empty like garbage. There is no gain for us to point out each other's mistakes. There is no victory in fighting each other instead of the real enemy. Direct your anger to the right place, sister."

"Wait," Zahra said, searching the faces in the room. "Where's Kobe?"

Kai dug his teeth hard into his bottom lip. When no one else answered, he said, "They took him. Deacon, too."

"What?" Lucinda said. She huddled around the young Shield Angels.

"Right. What's the plan?" Lionel asked. His top lip curled, and fire flickered in his palm.

Wyatt and Annika stared at each other as if trying to read the other's thoughts. Kai squeezed Eden's hand, resisting the urge to knock their heads together. Eventually, Annika gave a slight nod.

Wyatt faced everyone again. "We prepare. They infiltrated our home for the second time, it's about time we returned the favor."

"Ha!" Kai chortled. Finally, they were all on the same page. "You should have done that a long time ago."

The icy stare he received from Annika was enough to freeze a volcano. Kai lifted his chin, standing his ground. He was right. All this time, he was right, and she knew it.

"How can I help?" Jia piped up. "I'm not an adult yet and if I get caught... I mean, I can handle another extraction."

"Stand with us, Jia." Wyatt waved her over. He thought for a moment before saying, "We'll need as many people as we can. Unfortunately, that does mean those who are at high risk of not surviving an extraction. So if you're not up to it, we won't frown on your decision to stay."

"Well, it's a no-brainer for me. I'm in," Kai said, energy surging to his fists. He pumped his heels up and down. So completely ready to punch someone.

Annika shared a concerned look with Wyatt. Turning back, her face was emotionless as she said, "You won't be coming."

"Pfft," Kai scoffed, rolling his eyes. "It's not your choice."

"Well, maybe that's the difference this time. Maybe things will turn out better if you leave the adults in charge of the big decisions. I deny your request." Annika's low blow hit Kai hard. He could feel her hate for him in every venomous word.

"I'm going," Zahra blurted.

Annika shook her head. "Ahh, I don't think—"

"He's my brother," Zahra pleaded.

"Fine," Annika huffed, waving Zahra over.

Sick of the hypocrisy, Kai stepped forward. "And Harper's my sister."

"Sit down, child," Annika snapped, blue eyes like ice. "Just follow this one order, okay? I won't lose my brother. You're no good to me dead."

The passion in her voice pushed Kai back. She was on the verge; he sensed it—she didn't hate him... she was genuinely scared for him.

"What about..." Eden gave Kai an apologetic glance, then stepped forward. "What about me?"

"Nope," Alistair shouted from the back of the room. "She stays."

Wyatt shrugged. "Sorry, Eeds, the Watcher has spoken."

Still hung up on Annika's admission Kai stared at her, waiting for her to return the look. He watched her move around the room, asking for other people to join them. She didn't give a single peek his way. Nothing. That was all she was willing to give. A sentence that somehow, in her own way, told him that she cared.

It was enough to give him pause.

"Come on," she called out. "Let's go save our families." And as she walked past Kai and Eden, she gave a quick side glance and commanded, "Watch the young ones. Keep them safe."

Yes. Annika was scared for her brother. She was scared to lose him. She was scared that maybe they'd stuff it all up and death would follow. What she didn't understand though, was that he didn't care. Kai was willing to make that sacrifice for the safety of their people.

35

Eden

Eden looked out the broken window and watched the Nephilim army march through a portal. When it snapped shut, she paid close attention to the remnant, hanging in midair. She watched it for a good minute, waiting for it to disappear. But it remained.

An open invitation.

The room was quiet. A handful of people remained. The Healer tutor, Scarlett, sat with the small children, distracting them with a game of I Spy.

Kai stood beside Eden, staring out the broken window. Tears deepened the color of his aqua eyes. The sight broke her heart. She reached for his cheek, breaking him out of his trance. He turned his attention to her and closed his eyes, nuzzling into her touch.

"Edie," Kai's voice was barely a whisper. "We have to go help them."

She waited for him to open his eyes again before she nodded. Fervently. Her whole heart agreed. "I know."

The gap between them closed as he bared his lips on hers. A kiss that felt both optimistic and final. She grasped onto his shirt as if holding onto the moment, willing it to last.

As he pulled away, he rested his forehead on hers, fingertips caressing her jawline. The beating of her heart vibrated through her body. His touch made her feel as light as a cloud.

"Malakai," she said, breathlessly. "I lov—"

"Shh." Kai pulled her in close, kissing her forehead. "Tell me later. After the battle."

The dismissal hurt; Eden couldn't understand why he didn't want to hear the words. What they were walking into wasn't favorable. What if there is no after? She knew what she was stepping into. Did he? "Are you sure you're okay to go?"

"I'm an Angel of War. I was born ready."

Eden nodded. She began moving for the door when Kai latched onto her hand, he tugged her back to him. Strong arms enveloped her body. As if reading her mind, he said, "There'll be an after, I promise."

They walked hand in hand to the middle of the field. The mid-afternoon sun lit up the treetops, turning the leaves golden—it opposed the darkness that had settled around their hearts.

"Are you good to create a portal?" Kai asked, rubbing the nape of his neck.

Eden pointed at the remnant Wyatt left hanging. She assumed he left it to make it an easy exit for anyone who needed to escape without him. "I won't need to."

Eden pinched the remnant and flicked her fingers apart. A portal sprung open before them. Through it, she saw a dark image—a wasteland surrounded a lake of mud, and in the distance, a city destroyed. It was desolate and seemed barren, nothing but a shell of what once was. Seven sectors, once brimming with life and love, now rubble and lifeless. Even in its desolate state, there was no doubting where they were.

Lumeria.

Eden lifted her foot from the lush green grass and as she moved through the portal, it landed on dry cracked earth. A smell like old, raw meat hit her like a bolt of lightning. Everything in her body told her to get out but her will was stronger. When Kai followed her through, she flicked her wrist and the portal zipped shut.

"Do you have any memory of getting to or leaving the extraction chambers?" Kai asked, eyes on the city.

"No." Eden swallowed, her mouth suddenly void of saliva. "I remember having a sack or something over my head."

Kai didn't say anything to that. He didn't need to. They both knew what had happened. The Hunters invaded their city and then in an act of sheer audacity used it as their secret base.

Despite the overwhelming need to purge the contents of her stomach, Eden took a deep breath and opened her wings. Kai didn't reach for her hand and she was thankful. There was something about the need to move with reverence through their homeland.

It would take almost an hour to walk from the lake to the inner city, so they lifted off the ground, staying low to remain unseen. Together they flew, wings beating in silence.

They reached the outskirts of the Warrior sector first. Overgrown weeds covered what was once lush gardens of vegetables and fruit and flowers. Scattered houses, most burned, surrounded the urban buildings and high-rises.

The closer they got to the city, the harder Eden's heart pounded. Flashbacks of her last moments in Lumeria coursed through her mind. Of her, Kai, and Annika flying frantically around the buildings, twelve years earlier. The sound of screams reverberated through her mind and she wasn't quite sure whether it was the memory or real life.

As the houses made way for larger buildings and

apartment blocks. Eden followed Kai, as he weaved through alleyways. This was his home once. The high-rises, once stoic and pristine white, now scarred with scorch marks and buckled doors. Blue-winged badges were marked on every corner, a symbol of pride and honor, were almost hidden under dust and overgrown vines.

Kai landed a block away from the epicenter—a large heptagon courtyard where all the sectors would come together for weekly gatherings and celebrations. Running, he waved his arm and called to Eden, "This way."

As they turned the corner that separated the Warrior sector and the courtyard, she ran her hand over the blue tag, letting her fingers trace the grooves. Kai stood in the middle of the once vibrant courtyard, nothing but shattered glass and burned trees remained. He slowly moved around with his ear tilted down, as though trying to hear something, anything.

With her hand still resting on the Warrior emblem, Eden closed her eyes. There were no screams filling her mind, only music. Violins, bongos, pan flutes. And there was laughter. Fairy lights hung from trees, placed randomly throughout the courtyard. Not everyone was dancing, but that was okay because there wasn't a single person left unsmiling. Even at an age younger than six, Eden knew then how important it was to be in a community of acceptance and understanding like that.

"Eden?" Kai called, his voice moving closer to her. "Are you all right?"

She didn't realize it, but she was swaying. Her head stuck in a good memory. Smile on her face, she opened her eyes. Kai stood in front of her, brows low. He cupped her shoulders, his expression deepening.

"I'm fine. Just remembering." Eden inhaled sharply. "Let's get our people back."

Nodding, Kai swiveled on his feet. "Do you recall some kind of underground network?"

"No, I don't think—oh, wait. Yes. There was a bunker wasn't there?"

Kai lifted his hands and clutched them at the back of his neck. His eyes lifted to the sky, thinking. "Something like that. Or... a..." He snapped his eyes to Eden. "A hospital. Where the mothers would give birth in peace."

Eden nodded enthusiastically and then her face dropped. "I don't know where the entrance—"

"Your watch!" Kai clicked his fingers at her. "Eden, for God's sake, your watch."

Muttering under her breath about how stupid she was, Eden lifted her wrist and flicked the projector up. Two blue dots lit up in the space where they stood, both shining brighter than they ever had. Eden zoomed out on the blueprint, searching for any others that might pop up. When she couldn't see any other light, she zoomed in again and swiped up, turning the blueprint sideways. The projection showed the vertical plan of the skyscraper beside her. Slowly she scanned down, underneath the ground.

Kai was right, there were pathways leading to small rooms, dotted throughout the area, more pathways led to bigger rooms, and as she turned to face the courtyard, right underneath the center, was an even larger room. In that room, a mass of blue dots glowed, some as bright as Eden, others a paler blue, some barely visible. Scattered between them were red dots, at least twice as many Hunters as there were Nephilim. The dots moved fast, ducking and weaving each other. Along the pathway to the west, a thick swarm of red was charging straight for the fight.

"That's it! That's them," Kai boomed. "Where do we get in?"

Eden found seven entrances, each sectors' main building had a stairwell down, all meeting in one convergence point in the largest room. She said, "They'd expect us to go that way."

"What about there?" Kai asked, jogging toward a

sewer plate at the start of the Warrior alley.

A quick search on the watch showed Eden a ladder, leading all the way to a small room on the east side of the underground hospital-turned-chamber. There were only a few red dots in a nearby room, along with faint blue ones. Nephilim, either just extracted or about to be again. They didn't move, immobile side by side as the Hunters rushed around them.

Fear gripped her as she urged, "Let's get in there."

Kai threw the lid away and began descending. Eden followed him, keeping a close eye on her watch. They found themselves in a storage room. Wires, tubes, and serums stacked the shelves.

The walls were faded and condensation dripped marks down them from the ceiling. It smelled like a mix of bacteria and blood. Eden wrinkled her nose and returned her attention to the projection.

Hunters in the nearby room stood opposite the two faint-blue dots, as though watching... waiting. It was the extraction chamber; she just knew it. Wondering who they were watching, her thoughts circled one word.

Pures.

She flicked the projection across to the main chamber. The cluster of Nephilim now surrounded by Hunters. There were two options, to fight the hoard and save hundreds, or to risk the extraction chamber and save two.

Alistair's warning echoed in her mind. No one except Kai had ever survived three extractions, let alone four. There was no way, she'd let him take that risk. It was bad enough they were all here.

"See here." Eden showed Kai, hating herself for the lie she was about to tell. "I think we need to separate."

"That's not a great—"

She knew it wasn't a great idea. But it was the only option to have the chance to save everyone. On the verge of tears, she interrupted him, "We need to find Harper and Deacon and Kobe. We'll cover more ground this way."

"Edie?" There was pain in his voice. "We're better together. Show me the watch."

He clutched her wrist and yanked it high so he could see the projection. The Hunters in the main chamber tore between a mass of Nephilim huddled together. Blue dots scattered out, as though running for their lives. Every now and then, a Hunter would come close to a Nephilim and their blue light dimmed.

"It looks like they're cuffing them with the energy dampeners," Eden stated.

"Right." Kai dropped her hand. He ran to the door and stopped when he realized she wasn't following. Turning around he said, "We need to help them."

Eden squeezed her eyes shut in a long blink. Looking at him again, she said, "You go help them. I'll search for anyone left in other rooms."

Kai's shoulders slumped, the curves of his muscles tightening with held breath. Aqua eyes darkened as he let out a sigh. "Fine. If that's what you think is best."

The sadness in his expression broke Eden's heart. It took her back six years, where their reckless abandon wound up getting them captured. She wouldn't let him go back then when he was shot with a harpoon. There was no circumstance where her actions would have been different. She'd go anywhere for him. And it was obvious he'd do the same for her. He had already. He got caught for the third time and extracted, just because he went out and looked for her. It can't happen again. It won't. Not on her watch.

Holding her chin high, she removed all emotion from her face. "Yes," she said blankly. "It's what's best."

His chest rose and fell in quick succession, glaring at her in disbelief. A moment passed and his eyes lifted to the ceiling, and as his gaze returned, he nodded once. "Be careful," he rushed the words and tore down the corridor.

Hand to her heart, Eden took a moment to steady

her breath. She just needed to keep him away from the extraction chambers long enough for her to destroy them. Besides, fighting suited him. It's who he was.

Eden tucked a stray hair behind her ear and inhaled. She lifted her hand and moved the projection's blueprint back to her spot and focused on the next room. The Hunters were gone. Just. They ran down the corridor toward the main fight.

That was her moment. She portalled herself into the next room.

A feeling of angst and despair bubbled beneath the surface. At once, the familiar surroundings hit her. The room was cleaner than the other. White walls as fresh as the day they were attacked. Chrome tanks lined the far wall, their glass doors showcasing rows of small vials filled with grace—gold like the rays of the sun. When she was trapped behind glass, she remembered staring at that space to avoid the sight of Kai's fear-stricken eyes. Which meant the extraction cylinders were behind her.

She took a breath and turned.

The sight almost killed her.

Two glass cylinders side by side. Thick tubes and wires hung between Nephilim and a vital machine.

Both cylinders held two very different visions.

One, with Deacon inside. Red eyes and tear-stained cheeks, screaming as though his insides were breaking. His heartbeat flashed on the vital machine, pumping with what seemed like a million beats per second.

And the other, with Kobe. A cloudy liquid covered his limp body, globs of blood floating from his nose. Eyes open but lifeless. And the vital machine was silent. Just like Eden's gasp.

36

Eden & Kai

Kai ran down the corridor that led to the main chamber. He hated separating from Eden, but she was acting strange and a little defiant. He wanted to trust her, but something didn't feel quite right.

The closer he got to the others, though, the better he felt about the decision. It sounded frantic. An uneasy mix of desperate pleas and war cries.

As he approached the chamber, he slowed, taking a moment to get a grip on the surroundings. He stood in the doorway, hand clasping the doorframe, and peered inside. The area was large like it used to be an atrium or foyer. The space reached up beyond a normal ceiling at least five stories high. Broken fairy lights ran around the edges of the lower mezzanine and sandstone walls with golden architraves hid behind streaks of mold, small hints of a life now gone. Lining the far side of the wall were levels and levels of cages, each barely two meters squared. The cages stacked upon each other, at least twenty across and the same amount again above. Hundreds of Nephilim trapped inside.

Jia and Wyatt were at the fifth level, flying up cage by cage, unlocking them. Each time they broke a cage open, they'd either portal the Nephilim to the ground or portal them through to New Sanctuary. It seemed to Kai, their decision was based on strength and memory.

On the ground, Nephilim were scattered by the Hunters. Some left hopeless, constrained by clasps. Others, fighting with all their training to bring them down.

Shifters chose the strongest animals like lions and bears. Kai noticed a wolf that looked a lot like Zahra, ripping out the neck of a Hunter. When he fell down, she moved swiftly to the next.

Kai spotted Annika as she fought with rage, steaming toward a Hunter who'd just snapped a clasp over a young Healer's wrist. She threw the Hunter at another, letting them both crash to the ground. Embracing the Healer, Annika snapped the clasp in half and pointed to the back of the room. As the Healer ran in the direction Annika pointed, Kai noticed a small Shield, barely twelve years old, standing in front of a huddle of injured and clasped Nephilim, covering them in a transparent dome.

A surge of power sparked from his core, it sent electric waves through his body. He lurched forward into the room, ready to fight.

Insides churning, Eden ran to the cylinder. She smacked her fist against the glass, screaming as though her voice alone could heal him. "Kobe!"

How could this happen? If they had just let her go earlier, maybe they could have stopped it before—

How would she tell Zahra?

Tears burned the corners of her eyes. It didn't look right, the way his body floated, the way his eyes stared blankly right at her—his warming expression, gone. Forever.

Oh God.

"Kobe!" she cried again.

"He's dead," Deacon said. His voice was emotionless but his body said otherwise. His palms spread against the glass as his knees shook beneath his cowering body.

Eden shifted to him. It took a while for her brain to recognize that Deacon hadn't been extracted yet. She bounded to his cylinder, looking for a handle or button to press to let him free. There were too many buttons on the vital machine, she didn't want to risk pressing the wrong one. A crack where the door would have teased her, she scratched at it, panicking.

Deacon kept his eyes on Kobe as he said, "It's the black one."

On the side of the cylinder, right next to the vital machine, was a black button. Eden slammed her fist onto it. The door hissed and the cylinder popped open. Deacon turned to her, blinking slowly, as though detached from his mind and body. He was half-naked, clad only in a pair of Lycra shorts. He looked so vulnerable, tubes digging into the veins on his arms and legs. Eden ripped them out one by one and when he was clear, she took his hand, leading him out.

Emotionless, he said, "Do you think this is how my brother died, too?"

Eden didn't want to think about it. She didn't want to think about Kobe, either. She couldn't crumble. Not now. Not with how close they were. They would either lose it all or gain it all, the scales of war had no mercy. Her priority needed to be the same as it had been—to save her kind.

Deacon was in no state to fight. Eden pressed her hands together and opened a portal to New Sanctuary. Through the portal, Scarlett looked up over the heads of the children gathered around her.

Pointing wildly, Eden said to Deacon, "Go home."

He blinked once and glanced at the inviting barn. "I loved him."

"I know," Eden said, trying not to cry. "He loved you, too."

"Kobe, I mean. I loved him."

Eden placed a gentle hand on his back and whispered, "I know. We all did."

When his eyes met hers again, he nodded. Scarlett ran to the other side of the portal, taking Deacon's hand as he stepped through. When he was safe in Scarlett's arms, Eden closed the portal, taking a moment to remove the remnant.

As Kai ran into the chamber, Annika's eyes landed on him. He waited for her frown. But instead, her face lit with relief. She jerked her head, motioning him to join her.

"I'm not sorry, Annie. I had to."

Annika grabbed his hand and squeezed. Then, she pointed to the remaining Hunters, six of them, "Three each. Let's go, brother."

Kai nodded, letting his power rise. With clenched fists, he ran for the closest Hunter. It was easier than he thought. The Hunter had hesitated, frozen amid the chaos. Kai threw him to the ground, disarming him within a second.

He held the Hunter down, lifting his head to find another. One was a few meters away, gun firing constant bullets into a Shifter. The Shifter, a bear, remained stoic and unaffected. The bullets sunk into their skin, yet after a slight wince, they popped right back out. It was Lucinda, the strongest and eldest of the Shifters from New Sanctuary. The Hunter clasped his gun as Lucinda swiped his legs from beneath him.

Kai turned his attention to another Hunter, charging toward him. Annika side-swiped him, breaking his jaw with one punch. Behind her, another

Hunter crept closer, holding a clasp behind his back. Kai rose and thundered to meet him.

In one leap, he had the Hunter wrapped in his arms and they tumbled to the cement floor together. Gasping for breath, the Hunter clutched at his dislocated shoulder.

As Kai moved to finish him off, a sharp pain rattled through his skull. He twisted on the spot to see a Hunter standing over him. The barrel of her gun only a few inches away, blood dripping off its end. The Hunter hovered her finger over the trigger and squeezed.

Kai rolled to the side as the bullet whizzed past his head and lodged itself into the chest of the Hunter he just took down. In one motion, he took a hold of the gun and rose to his feet. Kai yanked the gun, claiming it as his own. The Hunter jolted where she stood, complexion turning pale.

A scream echoed through the chamber, resonating into the towering space above. Kai cupped his hand around the Hunter's neck, moving her aside to see better. Near the cage wall, a Hunter held Annika by the elbow, his knife dangerously close to her neck. Annika squirmed on the spot, clasp neatly circling her wrist.

Kai dropped the Hunter and threw the gun into his right hand. Without a moment to pass, he inhaled, aimed, and pressed the trigger. The weapon fired and a second later, the Hunter holding Annika hostage fell. The gun slipped from Kai's grip, hitting the floor with a clang.

And just when they thought it was over, more Hunters filed into the chamber.

Eden stared into the empty space, not wanting to face the sight of Kobe. The sound of war cries echoed down the corridor. Now wasn't the time to grieve. Sniffing,

Eden turned to the cylinder Deacon was in. She ran her gaze over the machine, the tubes, the controls.

No one was going to go through it ever again. She dug her fingernails into her palms and focused on the machine, intent on destroying it from the inside out. As she lifted her arms, she noticed a flash of color on her watch.

Two red dots and one blue came steaming into the chamber.

Eden spun around in time to face them. Two Hunters, one with obsidian eyes and black veins, held a Nephilim between them. Her hair was long and platinum, her eyes aqua like a shallow lake.

Harper wrestled against their hold, but it was no use, not with a bronze clasp around her wrist.

"What the hell?" The Hunter with black eyes gawked at Eden. He peered behind her to an empty cylinder. "Where's the pure?"

"Eden?" Harper cried, still wriggling and fighting in their hold.

"Take me!" Eden shouted. "I'm not a pure but I am a direct child of Azrael and I'm stronger than most Nephilim. You've taken me twice before; you must know how powerful my grace is."

"Will that make her more powerful than a pure?" the other Hunter said. As he twisted his head, Eden saw small streaks of dark blood forking up inside his neck.

The first Hunter shrugged in response. He tucked his hand into his back pocket and pulled out another clasp. "Why don't we take both?"

"I said." Eden felt her blood boil. Energy surged through her body. "Take me in her place."

The Hunter snapped to attention. His eyes glazed over and as if moving not by his own will, he released Harper and scurried for Eden, bringing the clasp close to her wrist.

"Wait," Eden said, fingers tingling, ready to send them flying. But she couldn't risk hurting Harper. "Let her go first."

The Hunter stopped and glared at his companion. "Go on, undo it."

"Dale? Are you crazy? Put the clasp on the bitch, we'll have them both," the Hunter scolded, keeping a grip on Harper.

The Hunter called Dale blinked rapidly as if not understanding. His left eye twitched and grasped Eden's shoulder. "I'm your senior, Josh. Are you going to go against me?"

"I... uh... are you sure?"

"Powerful trumps pure." Dale hovered the clasp over Eden. "Let the pure go."

"If you say so," Josh sighed.

He unlatched the clasp at the same time as Dale clicked one onto Eden's wrist.

In an instant, she felt her energy drop. All the buzzing that lived under the surface suddenly vanished.

As soon as the clasp was on, Dale shook his head. "What the hell?" He glared at Eden. "What did you do to me?"

"Eden?" Harper leaned forward, itching to fight.

"Seize the pure," Dale commanded.

"What?" Josh looked between Harper and Dale. "But... you said—"

"Run, Harper!" Eden cried. "Kai's close, he's in the main chamber."

"Seize. The. God-damned. Pure," Dale screamed. He yanked Eden by the elbow and dragged her next to the extraction cylinder.

Josh leapt for Harper, clasp still in his hand. She ducked his attempt and pushed him in the back, sending him skidding along the floor. As soon as she moved her attention to Dale, he threw Eden into the cylinder.

"Oh no, you don't," Harper screamed, running at Dale.

He slammed the door and hovered his finger over a

button on the vital machine. "Uh-uh, girly. See this button? Once it's pressed, boom, done. If you try to get her out, she dies. There's no turning back once the extraction starts. So, be a good little pure and back up."

Harper stopped in her tracks. Tears streamed down her face as she pored over Eden. "Why would you do this?"

An overwhelming urge to wrap Harper in her arms fell over Eden. This is what she was. A Nephilim. She made a promise that she would save them all and if that was at the cost of her own life, then so be it.

She placed her palm on the glass. "Go get Kai, he'll keep you safe."

Harper nodded. She scowled at Dale and ran.

"Heh," Dale scoffed. "You Nephilim are all the same. Feisty little fighters. Inevitably we win."

37

Kai & Eden

Kai watched more Hunters file in from the left of the chamber. One after the other, they kept coming. Through the doorway, he saw countless more, waiting to enter. Glancing around the war-torn room, the only Nephilim left standing without a clasp were Lucinda, Lionel, Zahra, and the Shield Angel in the corner.

Zahra ran to Annika, trying with all her might to break the clasp. But it wouldn't work, every time she touched it, her wolf returned to her human form.

"Everyone back up," Lionel commanded, stomping toward the ambush. He looked between Kai and Lucinda. "I need a clear path to the wall."

The wall was made of stone. Kai knew exactly what Lionel wanted to do. He nodded to Lucinda and they began running for the Hunters, still entering the room.

They collided with the line, right near the entrance and Kai pushed them into one another, back into the corridor. Lucinda took the other side, using her bear to give Lionel space. A posse of Hunters surrounded her, working together to clamp her ankle.

Lionel swiftly leaped between them, a direct line for

the wall. His fist connected and immediately turned to sandstone. He forked his fingers out and gave a cry. The wall shook, cracks splitting from his fist over and above the doorframe. He pressed deeper and the wall began to crumble.

"Get outta there, Kai," Lionel shouted, as small stones crumbled down.

Kai fell back into the chamber and watched the wall above the door crash down, blocking any more Hunters from coming in. Lionel swiveled around, fire lighting his palms. He set his sights on the remaining Hunters and threw his hands in their direction engulfing them in flames. Kai joined him, side by side bringing them all down.

When the last one fell by his fist, Kai swallowed and glanced around in awe. That was it. The Hunters were all accounted for.

"We did it?" Jia called, sending the last Nephilim from their cage to New Sanctuary.

A louder and more empathic cry bellowed, "We did it!"

The room erupted. Relief that it was over—that it was finally over—flooded through the chamber like sweet cooling rain. A few Shield's ran to the fallen Hunters, reversing their powers to hold them down. And the rest let their guards down in celebration, jumping and hugging and crying.

Kai ran to Annika and doing what Harper had done for him, he slammed her wrist against the wall. As the clasp shattered, he grabbed his big sister and tugged her to him, enveloping her in his arms. "That is what we're made for, my Warrior sister."

Annika pulled back, a look of fear falling over her. "Where's Harper?"

Panic hit him. On high alert, he searched the room, his eyes scouring the jubilant crowd. Across the way, right near the opposite doorway, a flash of platinum hair caught his attention.

"Kai?" A shrill cry pierced through the cheers.

He tore toward the voice. Legs feeling like jelly as he weaved around people. When he broke free of the crowd, Harper spotted him.

Kai's panic heightened when he saw her face, wet with tears. He took her in his hold. "Are you all right?"

"I'm fine," she said, pushing him away. "It's Eden. She's being extracted."

Eden eyed Dale as he pressed the black button and opened the door to the cylinder. Stepping inside, he reached for the tubes she'd pulled out of Deacon moments earlier. "Good thing your pure friend didn't realize I hadn't hooked you up yet. Her little fists looked like bone breakers."

Dale violently stabbed them into her veins, one by one. He pored over her, almost as if reveling in the pain he gave. He stood tall and grabbed her hair, yanking her head back. Leaning in, he whispered with glee, "Thank you for your grace."

Dale slammed the door and moved in front of the vital machine. He pressed the black button and the airlock hissed shut. His finger lightly grazed the button he teased Harper with, glancing at Eden and with a smirk.

Out of the corner of her eye, Eden saw Harper run in, followed closely by Kai. Two steps into the room and he stalled, eyes widening at the sight of her inside the cylinder. His gaze drifted along to the next cylinder, and his whole body weakened as he whimpered, "Kobe?"

Dale snapped his head around to Kai. "You're too late," he snarled, turning back to the vital machine. He lowered his finger onto the button. "She's ours now, not yours."

38

Eden

As soon as Dale pressed the button, a sharp pain soared through Eden's body. It started at the tubes entry points on her neck, wrist, and thighs. As it surged along her veins, agonizing pain filled every atom in her being. It reached deeper, further, hitting her very soul.

Eden screamed then, and as the stinging gained its peak, she felt as though she might explode. A moment of relief fell. But not for long. Eden felt not only her power leave her body but something else too. Her grace.

A harrowing cry expelled from the pit of Kai as he charged. Dale stepped away, facing the onslaught as if accepting his fate. Kai slammed into him, pushing him back until he hit the wall. Cracks splintered outward as Dale's head dropped. Kai threw the unconscious body, discarding him like rubbish.

He ran back to Eden, swinging himself around the vital machine. Wiping his eyes, he looked over the wires and buttons. His hands clutched either side, knuckles turning white. His chest rose shakily as he moved his hand to a red button.

"Stop!" Harper called. "You'll kill her. It's started, you can't stop it. She'll die if you do."

"Find Alistair," Kai snapped.

As Harper skidded out of the room, Kai pushed his fingers up through his hair, eyes falling on Eden. He moved to the front of the cylinder, staring at her behind the glass. Letting the tears fall, he cried, "What have you done?"

Eden blinked slowly and rasped, "She's safe. What about everyone else?"

"We've got them." Kai nodded. "We won."

"Goo—," Eden started, but she forgot what she wanted to say. "I... uhh."

"How can I stop this?" he asked.

She wanted to tell him that it didn't matter but she couldn't get the words from her brain to her mouth. A fuzziness settled in her mind. It was happening; she was losing herself. Her grace, her powers, her memory.

Kai, she told herself. His name is Malakai.

Eden stared at Kai's face as though it was the sunshine to cast the darkness away. She clung to his light as if she would drown otherwise.

The blue eyes staring back at her, hit her hard. They were clouded with tears, soul-wrenching, heartbreaking. She held on to the sight, willing it to remain. But it fell too quickly, like grains of sand through her fingers, gone before she realized.

Who was this boy in front of her? But more than that, who was she?

Shadows nipped at her heels. Its claws were out, scratching her soul as it climbed from the tips of her toes, up her legs. Her body felt as though it was floating, being held by the tubes that drained her entire being—drop by drop. Black circled her vision as she looked at him.

You won't take me, she thought. You won't get what you're after. You won't claim my whole being.

"Edie," the boy sobbed, his fist landing on the glass

that separated them.

Was that her name? Ugh, she couldn't quite grasp it.

She tried to reach for him, but her arms were restrained. So close yet so far. She watched him as he stared at her intently. A sense of something buzzed in her heart. She knew, whoever he was, that he cared for her.

"Eden," he begged, hitting the glass. "Please." His second fist beared down between them. "Remember me."

A vignette closed in around her. How could she remember someone she didn't even know?

"I love you," the boy cried. "I should have told you before. I love you with everything I have."

The words sounded like they should mean something, but Eden felt numb as they drifted over her like they were merely a wisp of air.

Still, she couldn't tear her eyes away from him. As the verge of sleep weighed down and the shadow clouded her mind, she tried to hold on. But she had nothing left. Her head bobbed, unable to hold on any longer.

The boy's eyes widened and his fists unfolded against the glass. Pressing as close as he could, he screamed, "Remember me!"

Then, the darkness won and swallowed her whole.

39

Eden

Eden woke under fluorescent lights. Too bright to see anything clearly. She lifted her hand to cover her eyes, trying to make sense of her surroundings.

"Hello, Eden," a deep voice rang out.

She tilted her head to see a man by her side. He had kind eyes behind black-framed glasses and stubble on his chin. The man glided his fingers around one side of her face and his touch comforted her.

"Take a few moments to catch your bearings. Going from last time, it will take a few days before your full memory returns." The man couldn't contain his smile as he moved to a computer screen. "Your vitals are great."

He moved to a steel table across the room and lifted a long syringe. Inside, a neon blue liquid swirled. He pushed the bottom of the syringe and a line of blue droplets squirted from the tip. Tapping the syringe, he moved to Eden.

She felt as heavy as lead as she watched him press the tip of the needle into her flesh. He pushed it deep into her vein and emptied the blue liquid. He cocked his head at her, eyes peering over his glasses. "Rest, now."

Eden blinked, tiredness seeping over her. Maybe she would just have a few minutes of sleep.

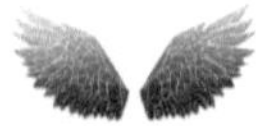

A constant beeping noise stirred Eden. She peeled an eye open, catching sight of the computer screen beside her bed. Within a minute, a girl rushed into the room.

Ignoring Eden, she went straight for the computer and pressed a button to stop the beep. She cried out, "Alistair? The serum has integrated into her system."

The same man as before entered the room and checked the screen. "Fantastic!" he said, smiling at Eden. "We'll have you back in no time."

"Remember me!" A voice screamed out.

Eden sprung up. The crisp bed sheets fell to her waist as she sat up. As the fog of sleep lifted, she noticed someone sitting in the corner of the room.

A girl with soulful Asian eyes leaned forward and smiled softly. She had a jumper on two sizes too big and her hair was the color of violets. "Hi, Eden, I'm Jia. We're cousins. Did you have a bad dream?"

Not quite sure if that was the case, Eden shrugged. She stared at the girl and opened her mouth to say something, but she didn't really know what she wanted to say. So, instead, she wiped her dry lips.

As if noticing Eden's discomfort, Jia lost her smile and stood. "Are you hungry?"

Eden knew what that meant. Yes. She was ready to eat. Again, no words would come, so she just nodded.

The kind girl held her hand out and Eden instinctively took it. They walked out of the room and down a long dark corridor. A dank smell seemed to come from the walls, it made Eden's stomach churn.

Soon, they came to a large area. Steel bars and worse smells. In the middle of the room, a large oval hovered, purple light surrounding the outdoors.

"What..." Eden cleared her throat. "What's that?"

Jia jerked her head as if in surprise. "Wow, it does work quick. Umm, it's a portal. It will take us to the food." She said "the food" in a singsong voice.

Wide-eyed, Eden moved closer. She took the scene in. A wide patch of green grass surrounded two barns, and beyond them was a mountain, too big to see the tip of. It seemed impossible to have a world inside a building.

"It's okay, it's better on the other side." Jia squeezed Eden's hand, then let go. She stepped through the oval and turned around. "See, come on."

Wincing, Eden stepped through, half expecting some kind of shock, but none came. She turned around, seeing the dark building through the other side of the portal.

"This way," Jia said excitedly, already steaming toward one of the barns.

Eden felt confused but also calm. She followed the mysterious girl into the barn. All eyes fell on Eden. People began smiling and tapping each other, pointing in her direction. A chorus of hushed whispers followed.

"I know you won't remember but they're looking at you because you're amazing," Jia said, leading Eden to a table.

"I..." Eden started, but she didn't know what she could say to that. It seemed like such a big word, amazing. She wanted smaller words. Like was she kind or impatient or clumsy?

"Yep, a lot of these people here are safe because of you." Jia slid into a seat and tapped one beside her for Eden. As Eden sat down, Jia continued, "Oh my gosh, Eden. I have so much to tell you and Alistair says to wait until you can remember but I'm just bursting."

Eden's eyes wandered away. She had no idea what this girl was talking about. She scanned the room, shifting her eyes to avoid the stares. There was one set of eyes in particular that she felt bore into her. Eden gave a shy glance to a girl standing in the corner by the door. She had dark skin and yellow hair that hung in ringlets around her shoulders. Her eyes were sad and bloodshot like she'd been crying for a long time. Eden winced. Everyone seemed to recognize her, but she had no idea who they were. She couldn't even remember who she was.

Void of emotion, Eden stared at the girl with yellow hair. Within a moment, the girl spun around and stormed out of the room. Eden dropped her head, fingers kneading into her palms.

She felt no guilt or sadness. She felt nothing. A numbness surrounded her as though she was only a shell, void of emotion or humanity.

"I got my full memory back, like you," Jia said, bringing Eden's attention back. "And I remembered something that makes things a little difficult, but definitely not impossible. Do you want to know why?"

Eden met her gaze. She wanted to tell her that she wished she'd stop talking and that she wanted to go back to that stinky dark place and curl up under the crisp sheets, but the eager look in Jia's eyes made her say, "Sure."

"So, yeah. Basically, everyone who was about to be extracted or had just been extracted were in the cages, a lot of us stayed there the whole time but some lucky ones were given normal lives, kinda like you, but with Hunters. Well, I guess that's still metaphorically caged." Jia reached to the middle of the table and grabbed a small roll from a plate that Eden hadn't noticed before. Jia tore a chunk off and shoved it in her mouth. "Oh, you want one?"

She grabbed another and held it out for Eden. Not wanting to be rude Eden took the roll. She pulled off a tiny piece of crust and placed it on her tongue.

"Anyway," Jia continued, waving the half-eaten roll in her hand. "About a few months after extraction, they send some people to halfway houses. And that's where they are kept, memory-less for six years until they wanted their grace again. What a pit, huh?"

Eden sighed and nodded. She repeated, "Pit."

The edges of Jia's eyes crinkled with delight. "Right! Luckily, Alistair managed to do a deal for me before my extraction this time. Phew... oh, sorry, not so lucky for you."

"Don't be." Eden shrugged. Because really, she had no idea what the girl needed to be sorry for.

Within a few moments, someone rolled a tray up beside them. They shifted bowls of spaghetti from the tray to the table in front of both girls. Eden glanced up and the words "thank you" rolled off her tongue.

The server gave her a sad smile and moved on to the next table. His hair was peculiar, all white. Eden studied the room, most people had a dash of silver just like his in their hair. Eden thought it odd but also it seemed important.

Jia rested her hand on her chin, a swoon-like smile on her face, and she watched the server make his way down the row of tables. She sighed and turned back to Eden. One slow blink later and she shook her head. "Anyway, what was I saying? Oh yes, so, all we need to do now is find all those halfway houses and get the rest of our people home. Once your back in full force, we'll be able to do that in no time."

Eden didn't know how to reply. Still numb, still so disconnected from herself.

After dinner, another tray rolled to their table. The server asked, "What's your favorite?"

Eden frowned; how would she know what her favorite was if she didn't even know anything else? It was a jarring question, to say the least, she glared at the person who asked it.

A boy looked down at her. He was different than

the other one, his hair pure brown. He winked at Eden with his turquoise eyes.

A spark, small yet significant broke through the feeling of numbness. Her heart skipped a beat. Something... she felt something.

She peered at the choices he held out for her. There were three desserts on a silver platter.

One was a brown rectangle, splattered with speckles of white. Another had layers, different shades of brown and white. Another was spongy, pink in the middle and red on the top.

The boy waited in anticipation,

She picked up the middle one, layers of brown and goo made her mouth water, even though she had no concept of what it tasted like.

"Caramel slice," the boy stated with a grin. He returned the platter to the cart and rolled it along.

She watched him walk away, taking the cart to the middle of the back wall. He glanced at her over his shoulder, his bright blue irises piercing through her. There was something about those eyes she couldn't shake.

Sighing, Eden lifted the caramel slice. She stared at the top layer as it melted over her fingers, and muttered to herself, "Do I know him?"

The spark inside of her burst open, shattering through the darkness like a lighthouse in a storm.

A memory rose to the surface. His eyes—they reminded her of a lake.

She dropped the caramel slice on the table and leaped to her feet, searching the room for the boy. She found him standing across the room, gawking at her. A smile flashed across his face, eyes lighting up. He promptly thwacked his hand to the door and pushed himself through.

Warmth spread inside her. She knew him. From somewhere, somehow she knew his face.

It stared at her, behind glass, begging her to remember.

"Sometimes, when the world feels like it's ending, it
is only just beginning."

ABOUT THE AUTHOR

Elle Scott lives in the Huon Valley, Tasmania, Australia with her husband, two sons, three cats, and one big ball of fluff, Labrador.

Telling stories has always been a part of her. When she was young, it was her dream to be a famous actress, and she would spend hours playing "make believe" with her sister. Her wild imagination turned everyday moments in life into extraordinary events. A long bus ride became an adventurous trek on the back of a horse galloping on the beach; or days spent in her backyard became days in the African Safari! Her imagination took her from her warm bed into a world where humans can shift into animals. Her biggest thrill is taking her oddball dreams and making them a reality with words.

Elle also tells real stories for real people. She is a multi-award winning family photographer.

Elle hopes to one day run workshops for self-conscious women, to turn them from a wallflower into a wildflower and give them the confidence to chase their dreams with ferocity.